SPECIAL MESSAGE TO READERS

This book is published under the auspices of

THE ULVERSCROFT FOUNDATION

(registered charity No. 264873 UK)

Established in 1972 to provide funds for research, diagnosis and treatment of eye diseases. Examples of contributions made are: —

A Children's Assessment Unit at Moorfield's Hospital, London.

•

Twin operating theatres at the Western Ophthalmic Hospital, London.

•

A Chair of Ophthalmology at the Royal Australian College of Ophthalmologists.

•

The Ulverscroft Children's Eye Unit at the Great Ormond Street Hospital For Sick Children, London.

You can help further the work of the Foundation by making a donation or leaving a legacy. Every contribution, no matter how small, is received with gratitude. Please write for details to:

THE ULVERSCROFT FOUNDATION,
The Green, Bradgate Road, Anstey,
Leicester LE7 7FU, England.
Telephone: (0116) 236 4325

In Australia write to:

THE ULVERSCROFT FOUNDATION,
c/o The Royal Australian College of Ophthalmologists,
27, Commonwealth Street, Sydney,
N.S.W. 2010.

ANOTHER SORT OF TRUTH

Valerie is delighted when her twin sister asks her to look after the children for the summer while she joins her husband abroad. She falls in love with the house her sister has rented for them, but soon realizes that she is being watched. Then, after a violent death in the area, Valerie knows that she and the children are in danger. Unable to confide in either of the men who are trying to befriend her, it is not until the mystery is unravelled that Valerie finds security and happiness.

Books by Betty Grass
in the Linford Romance Library:

LOVE ON A PLATE

BETTY GRASS

ANOTHER SORT OF TRUTH

Complete and Unabridged

LINFORD
Leicester

First published in Great Britain in 1992 by
Robert Hale Limited
London

First Linford Edition
published 2000
by arrangement with
Robert Hale Limited
London

British Library CIP Data

Grass, Betty
Another sort of truth.—Large print ed.—
Linford romance library
1. Love stories
2. Large type books
I. Title
823.9′14 [F]

ISBN 0–7089–5749–8

Published by
F. A. Thorpe (Publishing)
Anstey, Leicestershire

Set by Words & Graphics Ltd.
Anstey, Leicestershire
Printed and bound in Great Britain by
T. J. International Ltd., Padstow, Cornwall

This book is printed on acid-free paper

To Lea, remembering happy days in the forest

1

'How much further, Val?' the little girl asked anxiously 'I think I'm going to be sick.'

'Have a piece of barley sugar, Lisa.' Valerie tried to sound reassuring. 'We're nearly there. Look out for the signpost. It will be on your side — it says 'Greenleafe'.'

'That's not what the house is called.'

'No — that's West Lodge.'

'It's the name of the village, silly! I told you that before.' The boy in the back of Valerie's elderly Mini was fourteen — more than four years older than his half-sister, whom he regarded with lofty contempt.

'It's not really a village,' said Valerie, 'there are only a few houses: it's just a settlement in the forest.'

'Why did we have to leave Yorkshire?' grumbled Lisa. 'It was nice there.'

'Because the lease expired,' explained Richard, sounding unpleasantly superior, 'and, in any case, this will be more convenient. It's not such a long way from the airport and it will be a lot nearer your new school.'

'I don't want to go to a new school. I liked the old one. And I've had to leave all my friends behind. And I shan't see Anne's pony any more. It isn't fair!'

In her heart, Valerie agreed with Lisa. It was not fair to either of the children to be uprooted every few months, moving from one furnished house to another and never staying anywhere for more than a year. She could never understand why their parents did not provide them with a permanent home. Goodness knows, she thought, they have plenty of money! Richard and Lisa needed a proper home — somewhere to come back to during the school holidays, where their mother would be waiting for them. Instead, the family never settled anywhere, and, during their parents' frequent absences abroad, the children spent their school holidays in the charge of a series of housekeepers.

'It's a pity they're not dogs!' said Valerie to herself. 'Then, they could send them to boarding kennels.'

Valerie was an actress so, of necessity, she was something of a nomad herself. However, she had decided long ago that, if ever she met a man who meant more to her than her career, she would leave the profession and stay at home, at least until their children were grown up. Of course, this was only theoretical: she had never met any man whom she considered to be worth more than a passing glance! Now that she was nearing thirty, she doubted if she would ever marry, let alone raise a family.

'When is Mummy coming back?' asked Lisa, not for the first time.

'Not for a while, dear.' Valerie did not know. It had been a sudden impulse of Vanessa's to join her husband in Brazil, where he intended to take photographs of the wildlife in the tropical rain forest, to illustrate his latest book about endangered species. When she had rented this latest furnished house, on the border between Northamptonshire and Leicestershire, Vanessa had really intended to stay put for a whole year while Alex was abroad. But the call of the wild was too much for her.

Valerie was used to her twin sister's sudden impulses. She was surprised to learn, however, that Vanessa had been unable to engage a suitable housekeeper to look after the place while she was away. She was even more surprised when Vanessa asked her to step into the breach.

As it happened, Valerie had just left the cast of a popular television serial and was looking forward to a holiday. She was reluctant to do what her sister wanted until, realizing that the alternative for the children was to be farmed out with strangers, she allowed herself to be persuaded. Greenleafe, Vanessa told her, was a beautiful place and the house she had rented was quite perfect, but what tipped the balance was the prospect of spending so much time with the children. Particularly with Lisa, whom she loved dearly.

Valerie and Vanessa were identical twins but, although they looked exactly alike and had always been very close, their characters were different. Valerie had always been the more serious of the two while Vanessa could only be described as 'flighty'.

'What can you expect?' their father had asked their mother more than once. 'It was you who insisted on calling the child after a genus of butterfly! How can you expect her to be anything else?' He had been a naturalist, like his own father.

As children, Valerie, Vanessa and their cousin Alexander had spent many happy hours in the meadows which surrounded their family home. To begin with, Alex had collected butterflies — but it was not long before he had discovered that capturing the creatures on film rather than with a net was a far more satisfactory way to study these delightful creatures. The twins were glad to see the back of that horrible killing jar and took far more interest in what Alex was doing, though neither of the girls had any wish to become naturalists. Their happy camaraderie continued throughout their schooldays and Alex's years at university and was only interrupted by his sudden marriage to a fellow student. Unfortunately, his wife died soon after Richard was born.

Fond as she was of Alex, Valerie was surprised when his relationship with her sister developed into something deeper than cousinly affection. Alex and Vanessa were married on the twins' eighteenth birthday.

To begin with, the marriage had left Valerie feeling desolate — almost as if half of herself had been amputated. The bond with Vanessa still existed, but there was now a difference in their feeling for each other. Valerie realized that, for the first time in her life, she was on her own. She must learn independence. Perhaps this was a lesson she had learnt too well: perhaps she would never again be as close to another human being as she had been to Vanessa.

Lisa interrupted her thoughts. 'Is it an old house?'

'I think so,' replied Valerie, 'but I haven't seen it yet, either!'

That morning, she had collected the keys from Mr Wagstaff, the solicitor who was acting for the owner of West Lodge. Of course, he called her 'Mrs Markham', taking it for granted that she was the woman he had taken to see West Lodge some weeks previously. There was no need to explain that she was, in fact, *Ms* Markham, the new tenant's sister.

'I've seen it,' said Richard. 'It's not all that special. Mums and I went there at half-term. We had tea with the old lady.'

'Why didn't I go too?' wailed Lisa. 'I miss all the fun.'

'It wasn't your half-term, was it? In any case, you didn't miss much. Only weak tea and Rich Tea biscuits.'

'What was the old lady like?'

'Posh,' said Richard. 'And she had blue hair.'

'Now you're telling stories again,' laughed Lisa. 'She couldn't have! Nobody has blue hair!'

'What about Bluebeard?' asked Richard. 'Perhaps he was one of her ancestors.'

'I told you to look out for the signpost,' Valerie interrupted. 'It's a good job I happened to notice it or we'd have gone straight past it and missed the turn.'

'Sorry!' said Lisa. 'But why does Richard tell such awful lies? Who ever heard of a lady with blue hair?'

'I expect she'd had a blue rinse,' said Valerie. 'Lots of elderly people do. And Richard, you mustn't exaggerate.'

They had turned off the main road into a narrow lane, bounded by green hedges, and had crossed a bridge over a little stream. Then the ground sloped gently upwards until they came to a larger bridge with red-brick parapets, over a railway cutting. After that, the road climbed more steeply until they reached the top of a hill, where it forked. Valerie followed the branch to the left, past a low stone wall round what looked like a cattle yard. Inside were several wooden huts and a notice board by the entrance announced that they had come to FORESTRY COMMISSION. EASTERN CONSERVANCY: GREENLEAFE.

Further along the road, another notice informed them that no unauthorized vehicles were permitted beyond that point.

'Where's the house, then?' asked Lisa.

A man wearing a green shirt and khaki breeches came towards them and scowled at Valerie. He was tall and dark, with rebelliously curly hair and one of the ugliest faces she had ever seen.

'You look lost,' he said. 'Can I help you?'

'We're trying to find West Lodge,' explained Valerie.

He seemed surprised for a moment. Then he nodded. 'Of course! You must be the lady who's renting the place. Mrs Markham, isn't it? It's about two hundred yards further on, on your right. You'll come to a tall hedge, with an iron gate set in it. The house is behind the hedge.'

'I hope this is an authorized vehicle,' said Valerie.

'That notice is just to deter trippers,' he explained. 'The public are welcome to walk anywhere in the forest, but the Commission doesn't want all the rides churned up by motor cars.'

'Where is the forest?' asked Lisa, 'I can't see it.'

'You're in it!' said the man.

'Then where are the trees?'

The man pointed across the road to what looked to Valerie like an empty field. 'See those little green plants pushing up among the grass? Those are young trees. They were planted about a year ago.'

'They look more like cabbages,' said Lisa scornfully.

'They'll grow fast enough. It won't be long before they're a lot taller than you are.'

'Are you a forester?' asked Valerie.

'No. I don't work for the Commission — I just happen to be living on their premises for a while. Now, if you will excuse me, Mrs Markham, I have work to do.'

When he smiled, his face looked far less ugly. Valerie was acutely aware of keen dark eyes, staring into her green ones. Here was a man, she thought, who missed very little. Like Alexander. She was relieved when he turned away and started to walk off in the direction of the fork in the road.

They soon reached the hedge, with the iron gate set into it like a door. Through the bars, they saw a large, square house, built of the rusty grey local stone. Valerie gave a little gasp: it was perfect. She had often dreamt of living in such a house. If the inside was anything like — she was going to enjoy herself! However, Lisa was disappointed.

'It isn't old at all!' the little girl complained. 'I thought it would have lattice windows. And a tower. It's boring — like this silly forest. And ugly!'

'It's an old farmhouse,' said Valerie, 'not a castle.'

She parked the Mini at the side of the road and they all clambered out and marched through the gate. An old-fashioned bicycle with a wicker basket attached to the handlebars was propped beside the front door.

'Visitors!' said Richard.

Valerie took the key from her pocket but, before she could put it in the lock, the front door opened. An elderly woman, with grey hair and rosy cheeks, smiled and invited them in.

'Mrs Markham!' she greeted Valerie.

'I'm Mrs Gregory. I expect you'd like some tea after your journey. I've put the kettle on.'

'You must be the lady who looks after the house,' said Valerie.

'Yes. I come in three times a week. Mrs Spenser asked me to wait until you arrived today, just to make sure you got here safely. It will be a load off her mind when I write and tell her you're here.'

'Why — was she afraid we wouldn't turn up?'

'Not really — though there could have been a last minute hitch. I told her that wasn't likely, but she wanted to be sure. You see, she doesn't like leaving the house empty.'

'Of course,' said Valerie brightly, wondering why.

Richard chipped in. 'That was why she made such a thing about us being here all the time, wasn't it, Val? That was why she made you promise not to go away for the odd weekend, or stop out all night!'

'Mrs Spenser is a very nice lady, but she does have her funny little ways. Still, don't we all? I find it very strange that you call your mother by her Christian name, young man. I suppose that's the modern idea, but I'm old-fashioned.'

'She's not his mother!' said Lisa.

Valerie explained hastily that Richard's father had been married twice. She was beginning to have an idea why Vanessa had been so eager for her to take charge of the children while she was away, rather than a paid help.

'Come on, Lisa!' said Richard. 'Let's go and fetch some of our things out of the car,' and he dragged his little sister back towards the front door.

'I thought you looked far too young to be that boy's mother,' said Mrs Gregory, just as a distant scream announced that the kettle was boiling and she hurried off to make the tea.

Of course, Vanessa had said that she had signed some sort of agreement, undertaking not to leave the house unattended or in the charge of an employee, but it was only now that Valerie realized the significance of what her sister had told her. It seemed that she was not only expected to take Vanessa's place but also to impersonate her!

They had tea in the big, comfortable kitchen, sitting round a huge, scrubbed deal table. Mrs Gregory had produced platefuls of freshly baked scones and jam tarts, which kept the children occupied while she explained the set-up to Valerie.

'Mr Bagster takes care of the garden,' she said, 'and he comes in every day to see to the boiler, so there's no need for you to worry about that. He'll provide all the fresh vegetables you need — just ask him for whatever you want. I expect you'll want to do most of your other shopping in Stirbridge on a Friday. There's a very good market.'

'What about meat?' asked Valerie.

'There are seven butchers' shops in Stirbridge — and nothing to choose between them. They're all excellent. And if you want anything during the week, there are shops in Petercliffe. They're all very good, though there isn't the choice you get in town.'

'Petercliffe?'

'That's the nearest village, if you go through the forest. It's where I live — only about two miles from here. By the way, Mrs Markham, have you got bicycles?'

'No, only the car.'

'Mrs Spenser asked Mr Bagster to sort the bikes out for you. She thought you wouldn't have any of your own. He asked me to tell you that they are in order — he's put them in one of the sheds.'

'Thank you very much. They will be useful.'

'Mrs Spenser wants you to feel at home here. There are plenty of books, if you like reading, and up in the attic there are boxes of things the children might like to play with.'

'Toys?' asked Richard scornfully.

'Not only toys — all sorts of things. Fishing rods. Cricket bats. There's a croquet set, too. And lots of dressing-up things . . . '

'That's interesting,' said Lisa, 'what kind of things?'

'Theatrical costumes and all sorts of bits and pieces. Young Simon was mad keen on acting — he and his friends used to put on shows at the village hall in Petercliffe. They did *Charley's Aunt* and *Hamlet* — and several others. One year, they did a pantomime — *Aladdin*, it was. Simon was very clever.'

'Was he Mrs Spenser's son?' asked Valerie.

'Yes.' Was there a hint of disapproval in the woman's voice? She continued, 'His amateur theatricals were about the only thing he was really interested in.'

'What did he do when he grew up?' asked Lisa. 'Did he become a real actor?'

'I don't know, Miss. I haven't seen him for a long time, and I don't think

Mrs Spenser has either. I think he went abroad.'

Valerie thought it was time to change the subject. 'It's very good of Mrs Spenser to allow the children to play with her things. I know they'll take care of them.'

'Mrs Spenser likes children. She always has.'

'Have you known her long?'

'Oh, yes. When I left school, I went to work at the old manor house, where His Excellency and Mrs Spenser lived before they came here. When he died, she asked me to come and look after her. I was a widow too by that time, of course.'

'His Excellency?' Lisa was curious.

'Oh yes, my dear. He was in the diplomatic service. He was the British Ambassador in — I forgot where, but it was quite a feather in his cap. Now, if you tell me what rooms you want to sleep in, I'll go upstairs and get the beds ready.'

'There's no need for you to do that,'

said Valerie. 'You really mustn't spoil us.'

'It won't take me more than a few minutes, Mrs Markham. I expect you will use the front room.'

'Aren't there two front rooms?' asked Richard.

'Yes, my dear,' said the old lady, 'but the other one's locked. It's Mrs Spenser's own room — she's put a lot of her things away in it, so that they won't be in your way.'

'What sort of things?' Lisa was obviously intrigued.

'All sorts of little knick-knacks which might get broken if they were left lying about. And her clothes, of course — she didn't need to take them all with her.'

'And her jewels?' suggested Lisa brightly.

'Oh no, my dear! She's taken most of those to the bank, for safe keeping. It wouldn't be fair to you to leave them in the house while she was away.'

'So the room's locked up,' said Richard.

'That's it. Of course, I have a key,' said Mrs Gregory. 'I shall go in from time to time, just to do some dusting and make sure that everything's as it should be.'

By the time Mrs Gregory had made up the beds and had explained where everything was kept, it was time for Valerie to start getting the evening meal. Pleasant as the old lady was, she was rather a fusspot and it would be a relief when she left them to themselves. As she mounted her bike, she told them that she would be coming back on the Monday morning, just after half past nine.

'I usually arrive at half past eight,' she said, 'but I want to collect my pension first, as I've been away for a couple of weeks. I hope that's convenient, Mrs Markham?'

'That's fine,' said Valerie wearily. The children went to the gate and waved to the old lady as she pedalled down the road.

The house was everything Valerie

could have imagined: she had already fallen in love with it. She looked forward to cooking in that friendly kitchen; she had always wanted to use an Aga. But, for this evening, she had bought sausages, bacon and baked beans in Stirbridge and they had a fry-up, accompanied by thick slices of the fresh bread whose aroma had drawn them into a small baker's shop in the High Street. The sausages were delicious, quite unlike those Valerie could get from her London supermarket. She had bought them from one of the butchers' shops Mrs Gregory had recommended and she wondered if those from the other six were just as good.

Later, they all decided to go for a walk, to explore their new domain. Walking along the road, away from the forest office, they came to a sort of village green, surrounded by seven pairs of identical cottages. The verge was planted with ornamental trees, and they saw in one corner a slide, a sand-pit and three swings. A group of small children stopped playing to stare at them and a blare of loud music from one of the houses indicated that someone had their radio or television turned on full blast. Valerie was relieved that West Lodge was nearly a quarter of a mile away.

A little further along the road, they came to a wood. In fact, the road ran between two plantations of conifers. On their right, the trees were not much taller than the Christmas trees one sees in big shops. Planted in straight rows, at right angles to the ride, they formed a series of dark tunnels. The land between the rows had been cleared, but the remaining tangle of brambles and briers would make it impossible to pass from one tunnel to the next.

On the other side of the road, however, the trees were tall and thin and their tops formed a dark canopy. Beneath them lay a thick carpet of fallen needles. However, where there was a break in the canopy, where the light could penetrate to the floor of the wood, a mass of brambles had sprung up and, apart from several well defined gaps, the wood was separated from the road by an impenetrable tangle of undergrowth.

'That's a real forest!' said Lisa appreciatively. 'Dark and mysterious.'

'That's the sort you prefer, is it, young lady?' A man stepped towards them through a gap in the briers. 'Really, it's all forest. This is a working forest, a kind of wood factory. The trees opposite are only about twelve years old, while this plantation is over forty.'

It was the man they had asked the way to West Lodge. He had a nice voice, thought Valerie, but he really was incredibly ugly! Perhaps he would not look quite so bad if it were not for the scowl on his face.

'Do you work here?' asked Richard.

'Yes. I'm making a study of the wildlife. There are a number of different kinds of habitat, ranging from fields like the one opposite the office, to mature plantations like this one. The population changes as the trees grow, of course. As each area alters, the animals and birds gradually settle in the places which suit them best. When the trees are as old as this, very little can grow beneath them, except fungi. Next year, the whole of this plantation will be clear-felled and then the whole cycle will start again.'

'What do you mean, clear-felled?' asked Lisa.

'Cut down,' said Richard. 'They're going to cut down all these trees.'

'That's awful!' cried Lisa, 'Someone should stop them!'

'But that's why they were planted,' said the man. 'Trees are a crop, just like corn or cabbages. They have to be harvested.'

'My daddy's gone to Brazil,' said Lisa. 'He's writing a book about the creatures in the tropical rain forest. He wants to stop people cutting down trees — and so do I.'

'That's quite different,' said the man.

'When the Commission cuts down this plantation, they will plant some more trees on the land. And there will always be some part of the forest where the trees are just as tall as these — they all get cut down eventually, but there are always more to take their place. The forest isn't going to be destroyed.'

'Did you mention fungus?' asked Richard. 'Mushrooms? Or toadstools?'

'All sorts. And it will be a good year for them, too.'

'Poisonous ones?' Lisa was interested.

'There aren't many poisonous kinds here. Not many which are all that good to eat, either, though there are a few.'

'Can you tell the difference?'

'Yes. If you're interested, you should get a book about them. I'll tell you what — Mrs Spenser has a good book about fungi, with lots of illustrations. It's on the top shelf in the dining-room.'

'How do you know that?' asked Valerie.

'Because Mrs Spenser's a friend of

mine, Mrs Markham. By the way, I should have introduced myself before. My name's Anderson. Toby Anderson.'

'I see,' said Valerie rather sharply. Not for the first time that day, it occurred to her that Vanessa's charming landlady had arranged for several people to keep an eye on her tenants. Mrs Gregory had seemed almost too kind and friendly. She had not yet met Bagster, the gardener, and she was not sure that she liked the idea of him wandering about the house, even with the excuse that he was looking after the boiler. And now she suspected that Toby Anderson, too, had been told to watch her. She did not think she was being paranoid, but it bothered her slightly to think that there were so many eyes observing her — especially as she was not really the person they assumed her to be.

'Are we allowed to go in this wood?' asked Lisa.

'Of course,' said Toby. 'You can go anywhere you like. But I'd wait until tomorrow. It will soon be getting dark and you might get lost.'

'We'd better go back now,' said Valerie. 'We've all had a long day. There will be plenty of time tomorrow to go exploring.'

'I'll walk back with you,' said Toby, 'I'm going in that direction.'

'Do you live in one of the cottages?' asked Richard.

'No — I have a caravan. It's parked behind the barn at the back of the forest office. That's convenient, because I can run a power cable out of the barn.'

'Are you a gypsy?' asked Lisa.

'I'm afraid not, young lady! Nothing so exciting. I usually live in a house, but it's a long way from here — in North Yorkshire.'

'Oh dear,' said Lisa wistfully. 'That's where we used to live!'

2

Valerie did not sleep very well that night. Her bed was comfortable enough, though it was strange to lie in that big four-poster instead of the neat divan she was used to. The cause of her unrest was the nagging doubt she had about taking her sister's place and agreeing to look after the children during their school holidays. If she had realized that she was expected to *impersonate* Vanessa, she would not have been persuaded quite so easily.

It was difficult to understand why the owner of West Lodge should have made such a point of the undertaking by her tenant to stay in the house all the time until the lease expired. Richard had told her that the rent was low, even though it included paying Mrs Gregory and the gardener, but it bothered her when she overheard him warning Lisa that if anyone found out that she was not really their mother, Mr Wagstaff the solicitor would turn them out of the house at once. Then they would have to go and stay with his grandmother, and neither of them would like that!

Valerie also wondered why it was that Mrs Spenser had made such obvious arrangements for her to be kept under observation. It could not be because they were in any danger: both Mrs Gregory and Toby Anderson had told her that the children would be perfectly safe if she allowed them the run of the forest. There were always people about and, so long as they kept clear of the soakholes in the old wood — which were, in any case, protected by stout palings — they would probably be safer than in many school playgrounds! She had almost been convinced that the forest was a perfect place for them to spend their holidays.

She was slightly worried about Toby's remark that his home was in North Yorkshire. On the way back to West

Lodge, she had overheard him comparing notes with Lisa and had soon realized that his house was barely ten miles from the cottage Vanessa had rented in Swaledale. Valerie had never been to Yorkshire in her life and she had no knowledge of any of the places they were talking about so happily. Better, perhaps, if she avoided Toby, lest she betray her ignorance of 'the greatest county in England'.

It was a calm night yet, when she did finally fall asleep, she was woken up several times by odd creaks and groans. These, she told herself, were only to be expected in a house which must be several hundred years old. They were simply due to the effect of changing temperature on the beams and rafters; nothing to be afraid of.

The last time she awoke it was broad daylight and her watch told her that it was 7.30. She had a shower in the private bathroom which led out of her grand bedroom, noticing another door in its opposite wall. Curious to find out where it led, she tried it. Finding it locked, she concluded that it must communicate with Mrs Spenser's own room.

When she went downstairs to start getting the breakfast, there was no sign of either of the children. Hardly surprising, she thought. They had both had a tiring day and had been willing to go to bed as soon as she suggested it. She would let them sleep until their meal was on the table. However, just as she was chopping up some fresh fruit to go with the muesli, Richard came in through the back door. He was dressed in his favourite denims and a faded sweatshirt.

'Good morning, Mama!' he said.

'There's no need to call me that — particularly when we're on our own,' she told him. 'Have you seen Lisa? I don't expect she's up yet, is she?'

'She went out,' Richard told her. 'I expect she's gone to have a look at that wood. Shall I go and fetch her?'

'Yes, please. I don't want her to get

lost and breakfast's nearly ready.'

When Richard returned, holding his sister firmly by the hand, Valerie scolded the little girl for wandering off without telling anyone where she was going. And then, she had another cause for concern when Richard looked up from his bowl of cereal and asked,

'Who was that you were talking to, just now?'

'Just a man,' said Lisa.

'I thought Mums told you not to talk to strangers.' Richard sounded so superior that Valerie immediately wanted to take sides with the little girl, who immediately justified her lack of caution by reminding him that Mrs Gregory had said it was quite all right to talk to anybody they might meet at Greenleafe.

'Anyway,' she said, 'there was nothing spooky about him. He's a visitor; he said that he's staying in the village and likes to come up here for an early morning walk.'

'I'd rather you didn't go out by

yourself, Lisa,' said Valerie. 'Not for the time being — not until we all get used to the place. And this man you were talking to . . . '

'He was nice,' Lisa assured her. 'He didn't come from round here — he didn't sound like Mrs Gregory, or the people we met in the shops. I think he came from London.'

Valerie was washing the breakfast things when a man with a red face and ginger hair marched into the kitchen.

'Good morning, ma'am. My name's Bagster — I've come to see to the boiler. Thought I'd introduce myself first, in case you wondered who I was. Then I'll show you round the garden and you can tell me what veg you require for the weekend.'

'Thank you, Mr Bagster,' said Valerie. 'But is it really necessary to keep the boiler alight? The weather's so warm — and there is an immersion heater, I believe . . . '

'Mrs Spenser prefers me to keep the system going. It can get very chilly here in the evenings, even in the height of summer. And she doesn't want to risk the house getting damp.' Not to mention, Valerie thought, that the boiler gives you the perfect excuse to keep an eye on me.

The garden was large and impressive. The area surrounding the house was divided by tall hedges into a number of different plots. There was a rose garden, with an ornate bird bath in its centre; a long grass walk between wide borders of herbaceous plants; an unusual alpine garden, composed of raised beds and a range of old stone sinks and troughs, and one oblong expanse of grass, with a wooden gate at its far end.

'This is where the young people used to play croquet,' said Bagster. 'I thought it would make a nice formal garden, with a display of bedding plants in the summer — but Mrs Spenser doesn't want it to be changed. She thought your youngsters might like to play croquet and, of course, when her grandchildren come to stay . . . '

'Has she got a big family?'

'Only the one married daughter. The cheeser.'

'I beg your pardon?'

'The cheeser,' he repeated. 'She's married to some Italian nobleman. That's where Mrs Spenser's gone — to stay in their palace in Venice.'

'Oh!' said Valerie. 'You mean she's a marchesa?'

'That's right. I never could get my tongue round those foreign names,' Bagster said irritably. Valerie decided to change the subject.

'Isn't there a son, too?'

'Yes, I believe there is, but I've never seen him. By all accounts, he's a bit of a tearaway. Mrs Gregory knew him, of course, but I've only been here for five years — came straight out of the army. From what I've heard, young Spenser went abroad too.'

When he led her through the gate into a large, well kept vegetable garden, Valerie did not attempt to hide her admiration. Bagster was obviously an expert at his job. She asked for peas, baby carrots and plenty of salad greens.

'You'll be wanting some new potatoes, too,' he said. 'Next week, the broad beans should be ready. And there are still plenty of strawberries.'

'What happens to the rest of the vegetables?' asked Valerie. 'There must be far too many just to use in the house.'

'Mrs Gregory and I can have all we want,' explained Bagster, 'and so can that young man in the caravan. The rest go to the health food shop in Stirbridge. They're all organic — Mrs Spenser won't let me use any artificial fertilizers.'

There were flowers, too, in that part of the garden. Planted in neat rows, they were obviously intended for cutting.

'Help yourself to flowers, ma'am,' he said. 'Do you like sweet peas?'

Valerie had certainly noticed the cane wigwams near a sunny wall, covered with the soft pastel blossoms which were among her favourite flowers.

'Take all you want!' he said. 'The more you cut, the more they'll come.'

Valerie thanked him. 'They're lovely!' she said.

* * *

Later that morning, while she was writing to Vanessa, she sent Lisa, armed with kitchen scissors, to cut some sweet peas for the house. She came back with a huge armful of flowers. Richard was with her.

'Now we shall have to find something to put them in!' Valerie had not expected Lisa to bring quite so many.

'I know where there are a lot of vases,' said Richard helpfully. He fetched a pair of steps from the broom cupboard and they all went into the pantry.

'Mind how you go!' Valerie warned him. 'I don't want you to break your neck — or any of Mrs Spenser's valuable pots.'

'I'll be careful.' He reached up to the top shelf and handed down a two-handled pewter cup. 'How's that?' It tinkled as Valerie took it.

'Not big enough,' she said. She put her hand inside and brought out a key.

'What have you got there?' asked Richard. Then he chuckled, 'I expect it's the key to old Mrs Bluebeard's secret room.'

'Don't!' wailed Lisa. 'Oh, Richard! You are awful!'

Valerie handed him back the cup. 'Put it back,' she said, 'and forget you've seen it. It's none of our business.'

The sweet peas looked charming, massed in a deep, black pottery bowl with a metallic sheen to it. Valerie set it in the middle of the dining-room table. She could not resist burying her face in the mass of blooms, breathing in the wonderful scent of summer. At that moment, her happiness was complete. She was glad that she had come to Greenleafe. She no longer felt worried about deceiving Mrs Spenser: surely, it didn't really matter? She and Vanessa were, after all, almost like the two halves of a single personality; if there were any difference between them, she reminded herself that she had always been the more responsible of the two! So what harm could there possibly be in this little masquerade?

Her admiration for West Lodge increased. Behind its square Georgian façade, it was full of delightful surprises. The back rooms, including the kitchen, were obviously part of an older building, with low, beamed ceilings and lattice windows. What was apparently a cupboard in the corner of the kitchen turned out to be a narrow staircase to the floor above, built into the thickness of the wall. Above the kitchen were two empty rooms which, Valerie supposed, were once servants' bedrooms. From one of them, a door led back into the main part of the house, hidden in another cupboard beside the door to the room where Richard slept.

As well as a dining-room and a study, there were two sitting-rooms on the ground floor. The one next to the front door was rather grand. Valerie preferred the smaller, from which a glazed door led into a well stocked conservatory. It had not taken Valerie long to realize why Mrs Spenser wanted to keep her gardener — Bagster was obviously a treasure.

The only thing which irked Valerie about this idyllic place was the growing feeling that she was being watched. She resented it, wondering why Mrs Spenser had decided to take tenants at all if she was not prepared to trust them.

Lisa was writing a letter to her parents, while Valerie prepared their lunch.

'When will Mummy get my letter?' asked the little girl.

'I don't know. Probably, by the time it gets to Rio, she and Daddy will be far away in the jungle.'

'Then what's the point of writing it?'

'They'll be pleased to have it when they get back.'

'Why doesn't Mummy write to me?'

'I expect she has. The letter probably takes quite a while to get here. It's a long way to Brazil, Lisa.'

'Why do I have to pretend that you're my mummy? Is it because my real mummy isn't ever coming back?'

'Whatever gave you that idea? Of course she's coming back!'

'Then why?'

'I don't really know. Perhaps it's some sort of game.'

'Really? Richard doesn't think so. He says it's important and nobody else must find out!'

'You know what Richard's like,' said Valerie. 'Anyway, it's nothing to do with anybody else, so we might as well keep it to ourselves.'

'All right.' Lisa bent over her letter. A moment later, she looked up again. 'Val! How do you spell 'fabulous'?'

* * *

Richard was very quiet at lunchtime, but Lisa chattered happily about the plans they had made for the afternoon. They had, of course, decided to explore that fascinating wood, just along the road. But when, at last, Richard spoke, he said, 'We'll have to postpone that expedition until another day, Lisa.'

'Why? I was looking forward to it.'

'I was talking to a boy who lives in one of the cottages. He wants me to go and see him this afternoon. He's going to show me his ferrets.'

'I don't like ferrets,' Lisa said angrily, 'they're creepy.'

'That doesn't matter, because you're not invited. Colin doesn't want to be bothered with silly little girls.'

Lisa gave a wail of distress. 'Oh, Richard! You promised we could explore the wood.'

'Another time,' he said. 'We're not just staying here for the weekend, you know. You'll have to be patient.'

'We never do anything I want to!' said Lisa. 'You're a selfish pig.'

'Of course,' said her brother, 'so the sooner you get used to it, the better. Stop being such a baby.' He could be infuriatingly smug when he chose. Exactly like his father! thought Valerie, remembering how she and Vanessa used to trail about behind Alex when they were children, while he revelled in his male superiority.

'Can I go by myself then, Val?'

'I'd rather you didn't, dear.' Seeing how Lisa's face fell, and afraid that she was going to cry, Valerie scrapped her own plans for the afternoon and offered to go with her to the wood. Lisa cheered up at once.

'Thank you! And I bet we'll enjoy ourselves far more than Richard does with those beastly ferrets.'

As they entered the wood through one of the gaps in the tangle which surrounded it, Valerie noticed how the briers climbed high among the branches of the larch trees which bordered the plantation. How beautiful it must have looked when the wild roses were in blossom, the pink flowers glowing against the green of the conifers. She wished she had been there to see it.

She was glad she had brought a basket with her. As soon as Lisa noticed the many fir cones littering the soft, pinkish-brown floor of the wood, she started to collect them. Although she picked up only unblemished cones, the basket was soon full.

'Why are some of them broken?' she asked.

'The squirrels chew them up to get at the seeds inside.'

'What squirrels? I can't see any.'

'They probably ran away when they saw us coming,' said Valerie.

At that moment, there was a loud clatter in the branches overhead.

'Whatever was that?' asked Lisa, startled.

'Only a pigeon,' Valerie reassured her. 'Nothing to be scared of.'

In their progress through the wood, they had to make many detours to avoid the patches of bramble which had sprung up wherever a gap in the trees allowed the light to get through. When they had skirted a particularly large patch, Valerie noticed a small enclosure, protected by stout wooden railings.

'That must be one of those soak-holes we were warned about,' she said. 'We'd better not go too near.'

Lisa looked apprehensive. 'Are they really bottomless?' she asked.

'I shouldn't think so. That just means that nobody knows exactly how deep they are. Shall we start going back now, Lisa?'

'Not yet!' replied the little girl happily. 'There's still such a lot to explore. What's that?'

She was pointing to a tall wooden structure, about eight feet square. It consisted of a wooden platform, surrounded by a low parapet and supported by four long poles, joined together by stout wooden struts, some of which formed a rough ladder up to the platform. A crudely constructed roof, made from split logs with the bark still on them, surmounted the structure.

'It looks like an observation post,' said Valerie, 'but I've no idea what it's for!'

'Bird watchers?'

'Hardly! We haven't seen any birds, apart from that noisy pigeon: I think they all live on the edge of the wood.'

'It's spooky,' said Lisa, staring at the tower, which was reflected in a shallow pool at its foot. Further on, something else attracted the child's attention.

'Look!' she said. 'There's a hut.'

It was in the middle of a bramble patch; a desperately ramshackle shed, put together anyhow out of old planks, logs and what looked like broken-up tea chests. There was a small window, obviously salvaged from some demolished building, with one broken pane stuffed with old rags to keep out the rain. It had no proper door, but a hurdle covered with straw was propped beside a hole in one of the walls.

'Come and look!' shouted Lisa excitedly and, before Valerie could say anything to stop her, she had found a narrow path through the brambles and had darted into the hut. Valerie could only follow.

'Does somebody live here?' asked Lisa incredulously. Valerie looked round the hut. Along one side was a thick pile of straw. A big cardboard box in one corner was standing on its side, supported on four flat stones. It contained what looked like army blankets. In another box were a few items of crockery and a couple of old pans. There was also a picnic stove, which worked from a gas cylinder, and a small tin kettle, which Lisa picked up.

'There's water in it,' she said.

'Put it down, Lisa. I expect these things belong to boys from one of the villages. They probably come here to play. You mustn't touch their things. Anyway, it is time we were getting back.'

Disturbed by their discovery, she led

Lisa away from the hut as quickly as she could. She had no wish to be found there by whoever had left those things in that wretched hovel. It might belong to village boys, as she had suggested, but it was equally likely that some tramp, or an even more undesirable character, was sleeping rough in the place.

Getting out of the wood proved to be far more difficult than she had anticipated. They could not walk in a straight line because of having to dodge the bramble patches and, because the sky was now overcast, there were no shadows to indicate where the sun was. After they had passed the wooden tower, they became more and more confused. When they passed the tower again, Valerie realized that they had been walking round in a circle. A feeling of panic gripped her, though she dared not say anything for fear of alarming Lisa.

The third time they walked past the tower, Lisa said in a quiet little voice,

'Now we're lost, aren't we?'

'Not really,' Valerie tried to reassure her. 'This isn't a very big wood. We can't be all that far from the road.'

'Suppose we can't find our way home? We might wander round until it gets dark and then fall into one of those soak holes.'

'That's not very likely, Lisa. Look over there! There's a patch of light among the trees. I don't think we've been that way.'

'I think we ought to sing,' said Lisa. 'If we sing really loudly, someone will hear us and tell us how to get out of the wood.'

'That's not a bad idea,' agreed Valerie. 'What shall we sing?'

' 'Ten Green Bottles' is a good tune for walking to,' she piped up.

'*Ten green bottles hanging on the wall* . . . ' Feeling rather silly, Valerie joined in and they both sung lustily. They did not pass the tower again but she still had no idea where they were and, by the time they reached the end of the ridiculous song, she was beginning to feel quite desperate.

'*And if one green bottle should accident'ly fall . . .*'

'Pause!' hissed Lisa. She counted 'One, two, three' but, before they could sing the last line, a strong bass voice rang out close behind them, '*There'd be nothing but the smell left hanging on the wall!*'

'Who's there?' said Valerie. A tall, lean figure strode towards them through the trees. It was Toby Anderson and she had to admit to herself that she was very pleased to see him.

'Your son was getting worried about you, so I volunteered to come and find you.'

'We weren't lost,' said Lisa. 'It isn't a very big wood, is it?'

'Big enough,' replied Toby. 'It was a good idea to start singing — I was able to find you almost straight away. I'll take you home — I think Richard wants his tea.'

'Why can't he get his own tea? We've

been having a lovely time.'

'Have you seen any animals?'

'Only a pigeon. I hoped we might see some deer.'

'I doubt if you would at this time of day. They usually keep well hidden. The best time to see them is in the very early morning or when it's getting dark. That's when they come out to graze.'

'We saw a kind of tower,' said Lisa. 'Then there was a hut. Do you know who it belongs to?'

'Nobody lives in it now,' said Toby. 'Last year, there was an old tramp who slept there during the summer, but he went away when the weather started to get cold. I don't think he's likely to come back.'

'Did he build it?' asked Valerie.

'Did he *what*?' Toby had a pleasant laugh. 'I wouldn't call it a building — it's just slung together anyhow. I'm surprised it hasn't fallen down by this time. I believe some boys from Petercliffe made it. They used to spend weekends up here and pretend to be the wild men of the woods. That was a long time ago — now, they've both joined the army.'

In a surprisingly short time, they reached the edge of the wood. Across the road, Valerie recognized the green tunnels formed by the younger plantation.

'What's that tower for?' asked Lisa.

'When the deer are culled, someone sits up there and looks out for them.'

'What does 'culled' mean?'

'Sometimes there get to be too many deer and the farmers complain that they wander into their fields and damage the crops. So the deer control officer watches the herd and decides which should go. It's generally some of the older stags; any deer that don't look very healthy, and those with misshapen antlers. Then he goes up into the tower and waits for them to come and drink from the pool. When he sees one he's got on his list, he shoots it.'

'Oh, no!' cried Lisa. 'How can he be so cruel?'

'That's not cruel. He's an expert marksman and it's over so quickly that I doubt if the deer knows anything at all about it. And the rest of the herd take no notice at all; they just go on drinking or feeding as if nothing had happened.'

Lisa was now in tears. She ran ahead, obviously trying to get away from Toby as quickly as she could.

'Why did you tell her that?' asked Valerie indignantly.

'It's the truth. Would you rather I lied to her?'

'She's only ten — and she's a very sensitive child.'

'Ten is quite old enough to realize that being shot isn't the worst thing that can happen to an animal.'

'What a heartless thing to say!'

'Heartless? To help a child to understand the truth? Nature's not very kind to animals whose strength is waning or who are not particularly well fitted to life in the wild. Believe me, the man who does the deer control at Greenleafe is as gentle and humane as anyone you could wish to meet! You should ask your husband, Mrs Markham. I expect he sees things my way.'

'What do you mean?'

'He's a naturalist, isn't he? Like his father, the great Jacob Markham . . . '

'Yes, Lisa's father is a naturalist. He takes photographs of wildlife. How did you know that?'

'I'm in the same line of business myself. When Mrs Spenser told me about you, I did a little research.'

'But not quite enough, Mr Anderson. Alex's father wasn't a naturalist: he was an accountant. Jacob Markham was *my* father — Alex is my cousin.'

'I see. But surely, that's all the more reason why you should want Lisa to learn the truth about things, Mrs Markham?'

Valerie did not answer: how could she? Perhaps, if she had really been Lisa's mother, she might have seen things differently. But how could she tell? It was Vanessa who had married

Alex. She wouldn't have married him anyway, she looked on him simply as a big brother. So, if she had had a daughter of her own, the child would be someone completely different — not Lisa.

'Lost in thought?' asked Toby. 'When you've had time to think about what I said, I'm sure you'll agree that I'm right. But I'm sorry if I've offended you . . .'

'Not at all,' said Valerie coldly. They had arrived at the gate of West Lodge, so she thanked him for guiding them out of the wood and went into the house.

Lisa was in the kitchen. No longer crying, she was giving Richard a blow-by-blow account of their adventures. She did not mention the deer tower, but she told him all about the hut. Valerie was surprised how much detail she had observed and remembered.

'I might come and have a look at it tomorrow,' said Richard, intrigued by the idea of a secret hideout in the wood.

'Better not,' said Lisa, 'I think someone lives there. I don't think they'd want us to come poking around.'

'Mr Anderson doesn't think anyone uses it now,' said Valerie, 'so I doubt if you'd do any harm.'

Lisa looked doubtful. 'What about the water in the kettle?' she asked.

'You don't know how long it had been there, do you?'

'It couldn't have been there very long, Val. You see, it was still hot.'

3

The next day was bright and clear. Valerie was getting the breakfast, wondering whether the children would like to drive to Rutland Water that afternoon, when there was a light tap at the door. Not waiting for an answer, Mr Bagster strode into the room, his red face beaming. He was wearing his gardening boots, so he wiped his feet carefully on the mat.

'I didn't know you worked on Sunday,' said Valerie.

'I thought I'd do one or two jobs in the garden, while I have the chance. Mrs Bagster says she's going to wash her curtains tomorrow, so it will probably rain! I wondered if you'd had a look at the bicycles yet, ma'am. I think they're about right, but you must tell me if your little girl's saddle needs adjusting.'

Valerie had completely forgotten about the promised bicycles.

'Where are they?' asked Richard.

'They're in the garage with your car. You'll need batteries for the headlamps — though I don't suppose you'll be going out after dark.'

The children were already discussing where they should ride that afternoon, and, as soon as they had finished their breakfast, they hurried out to look at the machines. So much for the picnic at Rutland Water! Valerie was clearing away the breakfast things when Lisa came back, beaming with pleasure.

'They're lovely, Val! Not at all old-fashioned, and Richard's has got a dynamo. It works, too. Come and have a look at them. Wasn't it nice of old Mrs Bluebeard to let us borrow them?'

'You really mustn't call her that, Lisa — it's rude. Help me with this drying up and I will come and see them.'

By the time they reached the garage — actually, a converted barn — Richard had already gone, probably to visit his friend Colin. The two remaining cycles were ladies' models and Valerie was glad to see that Mr Bagster had adjusted Lisa's saddle to the correct height. He was obviously an efficient observer. Sometimes, she thought wryly, surveillance had its uses!

'Let's go for a ride!' suggested Lisa.

Why not? although Valerie did feel slightly nervous — it was so long since she had ridden a bicycle. However, after a wobbly start, the knack returned. As they passed the forest office, Toby Anderson was just coming through the gate. Lisa charged ahead, ringing her bell, but Valerie braked so sharply that she nearly fell off her machine.

'Steady!' said Toby, laughing. 'You nearly ran me over!'

'I didn't realize you were there.'

'At least, you haven't fallen off and hurt yourself. Where are you going?'

'Just having a ride round. Where does this road lead to?'

'Petercliffe. It winds a bit, but it keeps fairly close to the old railway line.

After about a mile and a half, there's a junction with the other ride. Then you'll get to another railway bridge. After that, there's a gate. It's usually kept open, but it does mark the boundary of the Commission's land. Outside the gate, there's a small sawmill and a lane which leads down to the village. I shouldn't try to ride down it — the surface is terrible and it wouldn't do your tyres any good. If you stay this side of the railway bridge and take the left fork, it will bring you back here. It joins this road just beyond the green.'

While he was speaking to her, his dark eyes never strayed from her own. Valerie found his gaze disconcerting, almost as if those eyes were giving her a completely different message from that his words conveyed. She felt her face reddening; she wanted to look away, though she forced herself not to.

'So, if we carry on as far as the bridge and then turn left, we'll make a circular tour?' she asked, feeling foolish.

'That's it. Where's the boy?'

'He's gone off somewhere on his own. Probably to see a friend — a boy called Colin, who keeps ferrets.'

'That's all right, then. Colin's a good lad — he won't lead your son into mischief. Nothing serious, anyway.'

It had not occurred to Valerie to question whether or not Colin was a suitable friend for Richard. She suddenly felt inadequate, though she resented Toby's assumption that she needed his advice. He was taking his role of guardian angel — or gaoler? — far too seriously.

Lisa came pedalling back towards them. 'Aren't you coming?' she asked impatiently.

Valerie had forgotten quite how enjoyable riding a bicycle could be. Bowling along these quiet forest roads was very different from steering through the crowded streets of the town where she had last travelled on two wheels. At first, the road curved gently between tall trees. Beyond this plantation lay open ground although, across the broad expanse of rough, yellowing grass, they could see the green tops of recently planted conifers. After that, they passed stands of larger trees, although these were by no means fully grown. At last they came to the left-hand fork of which Toby had spoken and, just beyond, to the railway bridge.

They dismounted and looked over the parapet to the line below. The rails had been taken up but not the sleepers and the banks were overgrown with brambles and scrub. They saw a wicket gate near the bridge, from which a steep flight of steps led down to the track. Half a dozen rabbits were feeding on the banks but, as soon as they saw Valerie and Lisa, they scuttled for cover.

'If there are steps near the other bridge, we can probably walk all the way along the line,' said Valerie. 'We could try it one day.'

'What for?' asked Lisa.

'I expect there are all sorts of wild

animals living down there.'

They took the other road back to West Lodge, passing between plantations of conifers in various stages of maturity. The road curved gradually to the left, crossing several rides which were no more than wide grassy tracks between the trees. At last, they reached a T-junction, and Valerie recognized the road between the green tunnels and the wood where they had been lost the day before.

They had nearly come to the cottages round the green when Lisa, who was riding ahead, suddenly stopped and dismounted.

'Hello!' she said. 'Have you lost something?'

A young man was poking about in the rough grass by the roadside. He looked up, smiling, as Valerie approached. She stared at him in great surprise: of course, she knew who he was! After a moment's hesitation, it was clear that he recognized her, too.

'Well, well, well!', he said. 'Valerie

Charles, as I live and breathe!' He turned to Lisa, who was looking puzzled.

'Obviously your daughter!' he said. 'She's exactly like you. Well, my dear, I'm looking for my cigarette lighter. I think I must have dropped it yesterday.'

He had not changed at all: did not look any older than when she had seen him last. Just after she left drama school, Valerie had been lucky enough to get a job with the resident company in a holiday camp. Peter — what was his surname? — had also been a member of the company. He was the most handsome young man she had ever seen and, at the time, she had fancied herself in love with him. But that had been a very long time ago: she had not thought about him for ages.

'Are you still in the profession?' she asked.

'No, my dear — I gave it up. After that big success I had in the States — I expect you read about it — I'm afraid I lost interest. I thought it was time I tried something else.'

Valerie was puzzled: she was quite unaware that he had had any great success in America. She remembered that he had always been extraordinarily conceited. That had been one of the things which had helped her to overcome her rather childish infatuation with him. His vanity outweighed his talent in her eyes. However, he was still unbelievably handsome!

'I haven't acted for yonks,' he went on 'Unlike you, of course. I've followed your career with great interest. But you've kept very quiet about getting married and having a family. I'd no idea. What's your married name?'

'My name's Markham,' she said. 'Of course, Valerie Charles was never my real name . . . '

'And what does Mr Markham do? Is he an actor?'

'No. He's a naturalist.'

'Daddy's in Brazil, taking photographs of endangered species,' said Lisa proudly.

'So you're staying at home to take care of your mother, are you?'

'Something of the sort,' said Valerie quickly. 'But, Peter! It's quite ridiculous, but I've quite forgotten your other name.'

'It doesn't matter. I used to call myself Peter Franklin — but I've changed my name, too. Now I'm Peter Claythorn.'

'What do you do, now you've given up the theatre?'

'This and that. At the moment, I'm interested in antiques. Old jewellery, china, bric-à-brac, that sort of thing.'

'That sounds interesting. Lisa told me that you're staying in the village. Do you know this part of the country?'

'A school friend of mine lived near here: I stayed with him once or twice. It's a pleasant place to spend a few days. I plan to go to one or two local sales and, in the meantime, I'm enjoying myself walking about in the woods.'

Valerie noticed that he was wearing a

particularly scruffy anorak. This surprised her; she remembered that, at one time, he had been quite a dandy. He smiled at her.

'Excuse my 'mean attire' ', he said cheerfully, 'I've been crawling about in the undergrowth.'

'What about your lighter?' asked Lisa, 'Shall I help you look for it? I'm good at finding things.'

'I shouldn't bother: it's only one of those throw-away jobs. I thought I might as well look for it because I'd only had it a couple of days.'

'We'd better be getting back,' said Valerie. 'It's odd to meet you again, after all this time — and here, of all places.'

'Just as surprising as it would be to meet you in the South American jungle. Not your scene at all! Did your little girl tell me that you're staying in West Lodge? What's it like nowadays?'

'Why, do you know it?'

'I went to tea there with my friend.'

'It's a lovely old house,' said Valerie, 'I

think we were very lucky to get it.'

'Have you met the ghost yet?'

Lisa pricked up her ears, 'Is it haunted?'

'Of course not!' said Valerie hastily. 'You know there are no such things as ghosts, Lisa!'

'I don't know,' Lisa sounded doubtful. 'That might be why old Mrs Bluebeard's gone away. Perhaps she thought she saw one.'

'Old Mrs Bluebeard?' asked Peter.

'Lisa means our landlady, Mrs Spenser. I've told you not to say that! Mrs Spenser's gone to stay with her daughter in Italy, so don't make up silly stories about her.'

They left Peter still poking the grass with his stick, moving in the opposite direction from the houses.

'Isn't he nice?' asked Lisa, as soon as they were out of earshot. Luckily, she did not expect a reply. Valerie had mixed feelings about Peter. She wondered how long he intended to stay in the district and hoped that he would not try to frighten Lisa with stories about ghosts.

'Been talking to any more strange men?' asked Richard later.

'He wasn't a stranger, so there!' said Lisa. 'He's an old friend of Val's. He was looking for a lighter he'd dropped somewhere along the road.'

'He'd better be careful he doesn't set fire to the forest,' said Richard. 'The grass is very dry. Colin and I have been talking to one of the foresters — he said someone lit a fire in the wood the other day.'

'It must have been that old tramp,' said Lisa.

They spent a lazy afternoon in the garden. Valerie tried to read a book, but it was hard to keep her eyes open and, at last, she dozed off. When she woke up, Richard and Lisa were squabbling.

'Bet you wouldn't dare!' said Richard. 'You're too much of a coward!'

'No, I'm not!' Lisa sounded shrill and defiant. 'I just don't want to. In any case, we mustn't.'

'Who's afraid of the bogey man?'

'Shut up!' said Lisa. 'You're a pig, and I hate you.'

Valerie suppressed her desire to find out what they were arguing about and suggested that Lisa should help her get the tea. Richard, hands in his pockets, wandered off towards the vegetable garden.

That evening, the children decided that they had had enough fresh air and settled down to watch television. Thankful that they both wanted to see the same programme, Valerie put on a light jacket and went for a walk by herself, following the road between the wood and the green tunnels. After about a mile, the road petered out, becoming a rough, narrow track. Straight ahead lay a wide tract of land, empty but for a rough heap of stones, partly overgrown with weeds and brambles. Nothing to see, she thought.

Just then, there was a slight movement at the far end of the open space. Beside the fringe of bushes which marked its boundary, there were three deer. After that first movement, they were standing quite motionless, giving her the opportunity to admire their beauty. Then something must have startled them, for, as if responding to some signal, they all turned their heads towards her before bounding, stiff-legged, towards the nearest thicket and out of sight.

'Are they the first you've seen?' A deep voice beside her startled Valerie. It was Toby.

'I'm sorry if I scared you!' he said. 'How do you like Greenleafe?'

'Very much — except for one thing.'

'And what's that?'

'There are too many people keeping an eye on me,' she said, 'I'm beginning to feel hunted. Or haunted.'

'What do you mean?'

'There's the lady who comes in to do the housework. She's very pleasant, but it's obvious she has eyes like a hawk. And the gardener — he comes in every morning to look at the boiler, which is quite unnecessary at this time of year. Goodness knows how many hours he works in the garden, but he seems to be pottering about most of the time. And you keep popping up all over the place — of course, you're a friend of Mrs Spenser's aren't you? So perhaps you can tell me why she thinks I'm too unreliable to be left alone in her precious house? I assure you I'm quite domesticated and responsible, and neither I nor the children are likely to wreck the place.'

'Is that how you feel?'

'What would you expect me to feel like?'

'You're a very prickly person, Mrs Markham. Hasn't it occurred to you that Mrs Spenser might feel responsible for your welfare? You're younger than her own daughter; your husband's abroad, in a place where it would be difficult to get in touch with him . . . '

'Alex should be coming back in a few weeks' time.'

'A lot can happen in a few weeks. In

the meantime, don't you think he'd be grateful for someone to keep an eye on you and the children? Even if you are not.'

'I've always been quite capable of looking after myself.'

'This is a lonely place,' he went on, 'and most women would be glad to feel that they were not completely isolated.'

'Mrs Spenser was well aware that Alex was away. If she had any doubts about my ability to cope on my own, she should never have let us stay here in the first place.'

'Perhaps she had second thoughts,' said Toby. 'I know she wanted a real family to live in her house — people with children, and with some sort of stability . . . '

Thinking of Vanessa, she could not help smiling. Stability was not a quality that would have occurred to her if she had been asked to describe her sister. Although the fact that she was staying at West Lodge under false pretences still bothered her, Valerie knew very well that she was by far the more reliable of the twins.

'There is something which puzzles me,' said Toby suddenly. He sounded so serious that, for a moment, Valerie wondered if he suspected the truth about her, but he continued, 'I can't understand why you haven't gone to Brazil with Mr Markham.'

'Someone has to stay to look after the children!'

'Don't they have any relations they could stay with for the holidays? No grandparents? Haven't you any brothers or sisters?'

'I have a sister,' replied Valerie, 'but she's abroad.'

'I'll tell you one thing,' said Toby, his dark eyes gazing into hers. 'If you were my wife, I should have insisted on taking you with me! I should never let you out of my sight.'

Valerie blushed. 'Other people have different ideas,' she said. He looked away from her, embarrassed, muttering,

'I'm sorry — I shouldn't have said that! Please excuse me.'

Now it was beginning to get dark. Although Valerie would not admit it, even to herself, she was glad of Toby's company on the road back to West Lodge. A wind had got up, hissing through the trees in a rather disturbing manner, although the air was not cold. They walked along in silence until, catching sight of something by the roadside, she stopped to look, with a little gasp of surprise. Among the short grasses near the edge of the road was a constellation of tiny points of light — not bright, but glowing softly and steadily in the gathering dusk.

'Glow worms!' said Toby. 'There are generally plenty about at this time of year.'

'I've never seen them before,' said Valerie.

'There are probably hundreds more round here, but you can only see them where the grass has been cut fairly short,' he said.

'You're a mine of information!' said Valerie.

'Only on my own subject, I'm afraid. About most other things, I am most terribly ignorant.'

'That's hard to believe,' she said.

'Is it? Try talking to me about things like art, or music. And as for the theatre . . . that's a subject I know nothing whatever about.'

'Why the theatre?' She looked at him curiously.

'That's something which fascinates me. I can't understand how anyone can take on a character that's completely different from their own and convince other people — presumably educated, intelligent people — that they really are somebody else!'

'Only while the play lasts!' said Valerie.

'Then what's the point, if everyone knows it's just makebelieve?'

'It's — it's a form of art,' said Valerie. 'Acting's an art!'

'If you ask me, it's a form of lying!'

he said, 'and if your actors aren't intending to deceive people, what on earth do they do it for?'

She did not attempt to reply. What he had said was ridiculous, of course, but she had an uncomfortable feeling that his remarks could be leading up to something — to the accusation that she was merely *acting* the part of Mrs Alexander Markham, to whom his friend Mrs Spenser had let her home. However, he looked away from her, murmuring;

'You'd better go indoors — it's getting chilly now. Where are the children?'

'Still watching television, I expect. You're right, of course. It's high time Lisa went to bed.'

When they reached the garden gate, he paused to wish her good night before he went on towards the forest office. She suddenly felt that he was about to kiss her — and that she almost wanted him to! His presence disturbed her: and not only because she was afraid he might begin to suspect that she was not what she pretended to be. In spite of his ugly face, he was one of the most attractive men she had ever met.

* * *

By the time she was in bed, the wind had become quite strong. The house was full of strange noises — creaks and groans and tappings which she could almost believe were footsteps in the attic. But of course that was impossible: she had locked and bolted all the outside doors. When at last she was beginning to drift away into sleep, her bedroom door opened.

'Val!' said a small voice, 'I'm frightened.'

'What's the matter, Lisa?'

'There are noises!' the child's voice trembled. 'I think Peter was right. This house is haunted.'

'Don't be silly,' said Valerie. 'It's only the wind. All old houses creak and groan at night, and the wind just makes it worse. There's really nothing to worry about, Lisa. Go back to bed.'

However, Lisa would not be comforted. When Valerie told her again to go back to bed, she started to cry. It was then that Valerie remembered a time, a couple of years before, when Lisa had had a series of nightmares, which had given Vanessa many disturbed nights before she discovered what had caused them. Valerie had never been told what had given Lisa such bad dreams, but the memory made her wary of insisting that she went back to her own room. In the end, she allowed the child to get into bed with her. Not long afterwards, both of them were sound asleep.

4

By the following morning, Lisa's night fears were forgotten.

'Can we all go for a cycle ride after breakfast?' she asked.

'You can both go,' said Valerie, 'but I haven't got time. Mrs Gregory will be coming, so I'd better tidy up. We don't want her to find this house looking like a tip!'

'I thought she was paid to do the clearing up,' said Richard.

'So she is: but it's not fair to give her unnecessary work. By the way, have you made your bed yet, Richard?'

'Oh Lord!' he growled. 'You're worse than Mums.'

It was such a beautiful morning that Valerie felt sorry that she was more or less tied to the house. It wasn't just the tidying up; she had a good idea that Mrs Gregory would expect her to be at home when she arrived.

'Please go to the front gate and pick up the milk, Lisa!'

The little girl went off cheerfully to do this small errand but she was gone for such a long time that Valerie wondered what was the matter. Perhaps she had met somebody. She did not want to chivvy Lisa but, as the breakfast was already on the table, she decided to go down to the gate herself and find out what was the matter.

Peter was standing outside the gate, listening to Lisa's account of the noises she had heard in the night.

'I know Val doesn't think so,' she said, 'but you may be right about this house. I think it *is* haunted. Of course I'm not really frightened of ghosts, but I don't much like having them around. Do you think that's silly?'

'Of course not,' said Peter.

'I used to be frightened of skeletons,' Lisa told him. 'When people die, they turn into skeletons, don't they? I used to think that some of the skeletons walked about, trying to scare people . . . and others just lurked about, where people could come and find them and be frightened — and scream! I used to think skeletons were very frightening. I don't now, of course.'

'Of course not,' he agreed.

'Is there anything you're afraid of?' she asked.

Valerie's rubber-soled sandals made no sound as she walked towards them down the flagged path, and neither Lisa nor Peter noticed her approach. Curious to know what he was going to say, she waited for Peter to speak.

'Mirrors!' he said melodramatically.

'What do you mean?' Lisa was puzzled. 'There's nothing scary about them, is there?'

'Sometimes I'm afraid to look at myself in a mirror. I have a sudden feeling that the face I see won't be my own, but someone quite different. Someone who looks the same, but isn't really me at all!'

'Ooooh,' said Lisa, 'that really is spooky!'

'He's only teasing you.' Valerie thought it was quite time they knew she was there. She turned to Peter.

'You really mustn't talk such rubbish to Lisa, Peter. She has quite enough weird ideas of her own, without you encouraging her! And Lisa, I did ask you to fetch the milk. Breakfast's ready — and don't forget that Mrs Gregory's coming this morning.'

'Not until half past nine!'

'Mrs Gregory?' asked Peter.

'She's a nice old lady who's worked for Mrs Bluebeard — sorry — I mean Mrs Spenser, ever since she was a girl. She comes to help us look after the house. And she has a key to the secret room, so that she can go in and dust all the treasures.'

'I'm sure Peter isn't interested in that,' said Valerie, but there was no stopping Lisa, who went on, 'Although she's so old, she rides up from the village on her bicycle. Isn't that great?'

'Do come on, Lisa!' said Valerie impatiently.

'Yes,' he said, 'I shall have to be on my way, too. Thank you for finding my lighter. Goodbye for now, Valerie.'

'I didn't know you'd found his lighter,' said Valerie as they went back to the house.

'I picked it up yesterday evening. I got tired of watching telly, so I went out to see if I could find you. I didn't go very far, so please don't be cross! I couldn't see you coming, so I came back again. And then I saw the lighter. It was quite near the gate, lying under the hedge.'

'That's odd. I wonder why none of us noticed it before.'

They need not have hurried over breakfast. Although Valerie had imagined that Mrs Gregory would think punctuality as important in the scheme of things as cleanliness, if not godliness, she did not appear on the stroke of half past nine. At ten o'clock, when the woman still had not arrived, she began to feel annoyed. By half past ten, she had started to worry.

'Perhaps she's ill,' suggested Richard.

'Then I think she would have telephoned.'

'Let's go down to the village and find out what's the matter,' suggested Lisa. 'We can soon find out where she lives — it's not a big place.'

'Suppose she's already on her way here and we miss her? There are two roads to Petercliffe and we could easily take the wrong one.'

'I'll tell you what: you can take one road and I'll go along the other. We can meet at the railway bridge and then, if we haven't met her by that time, we'll find out where she lives and root her out.'

'Good idea!' said Richard. 'That's what we'll do.'

When the children had gone, Valerie went up to investigate the attics. The strange tapping noise she had heard in the night puzzled her and she thought she would check that none of the windows had been left open or had blown open in the night.

There were two large attic rooms in the front of the house. In one, she found a collection of travelling trunks, bearing exotic labels. Some were very large and all looked as if they had been well used. In the other room was a ping-pong table and many boxes of all sizes. According to their labels, they contained dolls, toy soldiers, model train sets and all sorts of other toys. There was the croquet set in its wooden box; another box containing clock golf, and assorted bats, balls, and hockey sticks.

But what intrigued Valerie were the cardboard boxes piled in one corner of the room, each marked with the name of a play. *Charlie's Aunt*, *Hamlet* and *Macbeth*, as well as several others. She lifted the lid of *Macbeth* to discover several swords and shields and a couple of bloodstained daggers. A collection of realistic looking drinking-horns, made of papier mâché, was tucked into a black cauldron. Obviously these were the properties for the plays Mrs Gregory had mentioned.

Valerie put the lid back on the box and started to check all the windows. None of them was loose; all had been fastened securely.

When she arrived downstairs, the telephone in the hall was ringing. Thinking it must be Mrs Gregory, she hurried to answer it. Instead, however, a distant voice asked, 'Mrs Spenser? I have a call for you.' Before she could reply, the line went dead. Then, after a series of clicks came a man's voice.

'Is that Mrs Spenser?'

'I'm sorry. She's not here.'

'Then please can you tell me when you expect her back?'

'I'm afraid not. She's gone away. We've rented her house while she's abroad. Are you a friend of hers?'

'I wanted to speak to her on business. Family business.'

'I believe that she's staying with her

daughter in Italy, but I don't know the address.'

'That's curious. When I spoke to her last week, she said nothing about being away. I have to get in touch with her urgently . . . '

'Then you'd better speak to her solicitor. He's in charge of her affairs while she's away and he's certain to know her address.' She riffled through the little book beside the telephone until she found Mr Wagstaff's address, which she dictated carefully.

'And the telephone number?' By this time, Valerie was angry; this man sounded so rude and abrupt. And something about his voice troubled her — he was obviously the bearer of bad news.

She was wondering whether to ring Mr Wagstaff herself, to warn him about the caller, when Lisa rushed into the house, out of breath and looking very frightened.

'Mrs Gregory's had an accident!' she panted. 'We found her bicycle near the bridge. She's fallen down those steps on to the railway line.'

'Where's Richard?' asked Valerie.

'He's staying with her. He told me to fetch you.'

Valerie got the car out and they drove down the forest road to the bridge. As they approached it, Lisa pointed.

'There's her bike. I found it.' This surprised Valerie, for the machine was lying on the verge, hardly visible above the tall grass. Richard was waiting beside the gate at the top of the steps. As soon as they got out of the car, he told Lisa to go on and see if anyone was coming up the lane. The little girl obeyed him without question.

'Why?' asked Valerie. Richard came close to her and said in a low voice, 'I didn't want her to hear this. Mrs Gregory's dead.'

'Do you mean she fell down the steps and hurt herself? She's probably got concussion.'

'No, she's dead. I do know what I'm talking about. You'd better call the police — I'll wait here until they come.'

'Why the police?'

'Because somebody's bashed her head in with a stone. Oh, Lisa's coming back — you'd better take her with you. I don't want her to see Mrs Gregory — she'd be dreadfully upset.'

Richard took after his father: both of them had an air of superiority which infuriated Valerie. However, she could not help admiring the boy's coolness and initiative.

As she walked back to the car a long, lean figure strode towards them from between the trees. A pair of binoculars was slung round his neck and he carried a small haversack.

'Is anything the matter?' asked Toby.

'Yes — there's been an accident. I have to make an emergency call. Is there a policeman in Petercliffe?'

'Sergeant Weeks lives there,' he said doubtfully, 'but he won't be at home just now. Best get to a telephone and dial 999, if you really do want the police. Why not an ambulance?'

Valerie did not reply, but asked if there were a call box in Petercliffe.

'Yes — right at the other end of the village. It would be quicker to ring from West Lodge or the forest office. Would you like me to come back with you?'

'I'm all right, thank you.'

'You're looking very pale . . .'

Valerie felt very pale. The thought of poor Mrs Gregory lying down there on the railway line had made her feel sick and her hands started trembling.

'Please go back with her,' said Richard, 'I'll be all right here until the police arrive.'

'You'd better let me drive,' said Toby, opening the passenger door and hustling Valerie and Lisa into the car. As he pulled away, he remarked, 'Your Richard's a tough guy! Now, hadn't you better tell me what's happened?'

'Mrs Gregory's had an accident,' said Lisa.

'Why do you want to call the police?'

'I'll tell you in a minute,' said Valerie. 'Just now, I'm feeling a bit queasy.'

When they arrived at the forest office, Valerie told Lisa to stay in the car while they went to use the telephone.

'Now tell me what all this mystery's about,' said Toby as they walked through the gate.

'Richard says that Mrs Gregory's been murdered. The children found her bike by the roadside. Lisa came home to fetch me and, while she was gone, he found Mrs Gregory lying at the bottom of those steps.' She repeated the rest of Richard's story, adding, 'I'm so thankful Lisa didn't see her.'

'How did they know whose bike it was?'

'We saw it the evening we arrived. We wondered why she was late this morning, so the children went to look for her.' She looked at him piteously. 'Oh — how I wish they hadn't. Richard's very grown-up, but a boy of fourteen shouldn't have to cope with things like that.'

'It won't hurt him. Children are far

tougher than you seem to imagine, Mrs Markham.'

Was he trying to reassure her, or was he merely callous? She felt near to tears when he suddenly put his arm round her.

'Come!' he said gently. 'We must make that phone call.' She was so glad of the comfort his support gave her that she leant against him gratefully. When they reached the door of the office, he eased himself away and led her inside.

It was not long before the police car, accompanied by an ambulance, met them at the bridge. Toby and Valerie had left Lisa in the forest office, where the lady clerk made her a cup of tea and gave her a pile of information leaflets to look at.

'Will the police want to interview her?' asked Valerie anxiously as they drove back to where they had left Richard.

'They might want to ask her a few questions, because it was she who found the bicycle,' said Toby, 'but I doubt if she'll have to go to the inquest. Of course, I expect Richard will have to give evidence. By the way, you'd better get in touch with Wagstaff. He'll want to let Mrs Spenser know what's happened. And he'll have to fix you up with another home help.'

'Surely that's unnecessary. I'm quite capable of looking after the house myself!'

'Of course you are — but I happen to know that domestic help was part of the agreement. Mrs Spenser was very particular about that, so she will certainly want someone else to take over Mrs Gregory's duties.'

'I see,' said Valerie. What she didn't see, however, was how it was that Toby knew such a lot about her landlady's business arrangements. He must be a very close friend indeed! She was becoming suspicious about his place in the scheme of things — his previous assertion that she was being protected did not ring true. And why had everybody been so insistent that

Greenleafe was such a safe place, so ideal for a young family? Now Mrs Gregory's death made her doubt that, too.

* * *

To Valerie's surprise, there was no major upset when Lisa was told the truth about Mrs Gregory's 'accident': she took the news very calmly. She had been far more upset, Valerie realized, by Toby's explanation of the purpose of the deer tower. She coped very well, too, with the questions the police asked her.

Valerie herself was rather nervous when the police interviewed her. It was a relief that nobody actually asked if she were Lisa's mother: it was taken for granted that she was. When asked her name, however, she insisted that she was known as 'Ms', rather than 'Mrs' Markham, explaining that she was a professional actress. She would certainly not have told any actual lies about her relationship to the children but she was still prepared, as far as she could, to cover up for her absent sister.

The police did not ask Lisa many questions, though they wanted to know if she had seen any strangers in the forest that morning. Of course, she had not — though Valerie thought it best to explain that, as recent arrivals at Greenleafe, most people were strangers to them in any case.

Valerie told the police about the hut she had seen in the wood, but they did not seem interested. Of course, they knew all about it, confirming what she had been told about the tramp who had slept there the previous summer. However, when she remembered the warm water in the kettle, they started taking notes again. When they left West Lodge, they advised her not to let the children wander about by themselves for a few days.

That afternoon, Mr Wagstaff drove out to see her. He was very upset; he told her that he had known Mrs

Gregory all his life. He promised Valerie that he would arrange for someone else to come and work at West Lodge, as soon as he had spoken to Mrs Spenser about it. He brushed aside Valerie's claim that there was no hurry — the rent included payment for help in the house, so he was bound to provide a substitute as quickly as he could.

'Of course,' he reassured her, 'Bagster will come in every morning as usual. Just tell him if you want him to do anything extra; I'm sure he'll be glad to help in any way he can.' And to keep an eye on her, Valerie thought suspiciously.

Richard went to see Colin when the police had finished asking him questions. When he returned, he seemed to know a great deal about what was going on. Apparently Mrs Gregory had drawn four weeks' pension from the post office in Petercliffe that morning, amounting to more than two hundred pounds. Her purse was in her shopping bag when the police examined her body, but it was empty. Nothing else had been taken: the keys to West Lodge and to her own house in Petercliffe were in her coat pocket.

Richard had also been told that the tramp had been seen again, not far from Greenleafe. Although he was known to be harmless enough, nevertheless the police were looking for him.

'Who told you all this?' asked Valerie.

'Colin's dad. The policeman in Petercliffe's a friend of his.'

Valerie regretted having to keep the children at home on such a fine afternoon — she herself would have loved to go for a long walk in the woods. After a while, however, she remembered that croquet set in the attic and they went upstairs to fetch it. When Lisa saw the boxes of theatrical props, she gave a delighted cry and went across to look at them. She opened the box marked 'Aladdin' and found a straw coolie hat and a number of paper fans, as well as a bag of imitation jewellery and another of 'gold' coins. She put on several necklaces and danced round, looking for a mirror.

'Take them off,' said Valerie. 'You can play with those things another day — when it's raining. Now we're all going to play croquet in the garden.'

'I don't know how to,' protested Lisa.

'Neither do I,' said Richard, 'but we can soon learn. There's a book of instructions in the box.'

As the equipment was quite heavy, they took some of it out of the box and shared the load. Richard took the box downstairs and Lisa followed him with a bundle of hoops. Valerie took the mallets, but she stayed behind for a moment to peep inside the box marked 'Hamlet' and examine its contents. She found a pair of miniatures, some gold chains, crowns, metal goblets and garlands of artificial flowers. There was an ornate book for Hamlet to carry when he confronted Ophelia, but there was no sign of the particular object she was looking for. She gave a sigh of relief: the last thing she wanted was for

Lisa to open that box and find Yorick's skull grinning up at her — that would be sure to give the child nightmares again!

Although Lisa had taken the day's events in her stride, Valerie became worried as bedtime approached, lest the little girl's sleep should be disturbed by bad dreams. She need not have bothered. Lisa went to bed happily and did not stir all night.

It was Valerie herself whose sleep was troubled. She woke up several times feeling decidedly uncomfortable and then lay listening for the odd creaks and groans made by the old house on the previous nights. This time, all was silent. Unnaturally silent? she wondered — and then felt angry with herself for being so silly. Waking again just before dawn, she realized that she had been dreaming. This time, the dream stayed in her memory.

It was about Vanessa, of course. Ever since they were children, there had been a curious link between them impossible for an outsider to understand. They had never tried to explain it to anyone else but had kept it secret between themselves. Perhaps it was because they were identical twins that, if Vanessa cut her finger, Valerie could feel the pain, even when she was miles away.

When Valerie had won her scholarship to RADA, Vanessa, who was in Thailand with Alex, had experienced an unexplained 'high' which, lasting for several days, had nearly driven the other members of the expedition crazy. Valerie, shortly before Lisa was born, had suffered from backache and it was only when the twins compared notes that she realized that her own body was echoing the discomfort that Vanessa was experiencing towards the end of her pregnancy.

What was the matter now? She could not remember much of her dream except, just before she woke, she had seen Vanessa's wide eyes staring at her from a dark green tunnel. Vanessa was obviously puzzled and frightened and Valerie wished she were not so far away. She wanted so much to comfort her, to assure her that, whatever the trouble was, she wanted to share it and help Vanessa overcome it.

'Don't be such a fool!' Valerie scolded herself. 'Daddy told you that it's nothing but imagination.' That was true: her father had refused to believe in any psychic link between his daughters and, of course, she knew in her heart that he was right. She and Vanessa were two distinct individuals. Whatever her sister might be feeling in that remote Brazilian forest, it was impossible for her mind to communicate with another mind, thousands of miles away. Valerie told herself that her dream was nothing to do with Vanessa. It was simply her own reaction to the unpleasantness of what had happened the previous day at Greenleafe.

5

'It's Mummy's birthday on Sunday!' said Lisa a few days later.

'I know,' replied Valerie.

'Oh, of course!' the child remembered. 'That means it must be your birthday, too! Can we have a party?'

'We don't know enough people to invite to a party.' Valerie had no particular wish to celebrate her thirtieth birthday, but she would have found that difficult to explain to her niece, who went on excitedly, 'We know quite a lot of people! There's Richard's friend Colin. And Mr Bagster — and Hilda.'

Hilda was the niece of Mrs Gregory. Only two days after her aunt's sudden death, she had started work at West Lodge. She was a pleasant, obliging young woman with an easy-going manner that Valerie found far less intimidating than that of her predecessor. Although Mrs Gregory had done her best to make Valerie and the children feel at home that first Friday afternoon she had the air of an old family retainer. This had been very disconcerting.

'Hilda might not want to come,' said Valerie.

'I expect she would. And there's Toby.'

'Toby? You mean Mr Anderson I thought you didn't like him.'

'He says I can call him Toby. And I do like him — he's told me so many interesting things about the animals in the forest. And there's Peter — I'm sure he'd like to come.'

'You said he'd gone back to London.'

'I think he's coming back,' said Lisa. 'I like him very much!'

'I don't want to give a party. Let's wait until your mummy and daddy come back from Brazil . . . '

'I shall give you a present,' said Lisa. 'I was going to give it to you anyway, but it will make a super birthday present. Are we going to Stirbridge on Friday?'

'Yes, probably. Why?'

'Because there's something I have to get. Don't ask me what it is — it's a secret.'

'All right. Lisa — you just said that Mr Anderson talks to you about animals. When do you see him?'

'He often comes into the garden when I'm playing. He comes to see Mr Bagster. And afterwards he talks to me.'

'I had no idea!' Valerie was taken aback. She understood that Toby was engaged on some research project, which, no doubt, occupied much of his time. So how could he possibly find time to hang about West Lodge? And did she really want him to talk to Lisa?

Her thoughts were interrupted by the arrival of Richard, who was in quite a fever of excitement.

'The police have arrested somebody!' he said. 'Mr Bagster's quite sure they've got the wrong man, though.'

'Is Mr Bagster in the garden now?'

'Yes, of course he is. Why don't you go and ask him about it?'

According to the indignant Bagster, the man had not actually been arrested but was 'helping the police with their enquiries'. He was glad to explain to Valerie why he was so sure that they had got hold of the wrong man.

'Old Jim would never hurt a fly!' he said angrily. He was speaking of the tramp who had lived rough in the woods the previous summer: the police had picked him up a few miles beyond Stirbridge. Apart from a five pound note in his pocket — given to him, he said, by a gentleman — there was no sign of the money stolen from Mrs Gregory and he swore that he had been nowhere near Greenleafe for many months.

'Perhaps he was desperate,' suggested Valerie, 'and there's been plenty of time for him to have spent most of the money.'

'No — not old Jim,' said Bagster. 'He

never stole anything in his life, least of all money. He hasn't much use for it — he knows he'll get a cup of tea or a bite to eat, wherever he goes.'

The tramp, Bagster explained, had always been a popular figure in the district. Nobody knew where he came from originally, but it was rumoured that he was an educated man. During the months when he had been sleeping in that hut in the wood, it had been his self-appointed task to patrol the main road between the Greenleafe turn and the next village, picking up all the litter in a sack and taking it to the council tip, over a mile away. Since he had left the neighbourhood, that stretch of road had been much less tidy.

'Why did he go away?' asked Valerie.

'One of the young foresters complained about him living in the wood. Threatened to pull down the hut. Jim didn't want to cause trouble, so he left.'

'In any case, the winter was coming on,' said a deep voice behind her. Valerie swivelled round to see Toby, leaning against an apple tree.

'How long have you been there?' she asked accusingly.

'Long enough. I wanted to have a word with you, *Ms* Markham.' He emphasized 'Ms' in a very irritating way.

'I'll get along to the potting shed and have my tea, then.' Bagster picked up his trug and walked away down the path.

'What have you to say, then?' asked Valerie.

'I wondered if you had heard from Mrs Spenser since she went away.'

'No. Why should I have done?'

'She might have written to you. According to Wagstaff, she took quite a fancy to that boy of yours. She could have been in touch.'

'Even if she had, what concern is it of yours?'

'I told you — she's a friend of mine.'

'So?'

'I wonder if you have any idea where she is.'

'I thought she was staying with her daughter, in Italy. Mr Wagstaff knows her address. He said he was getting in touch with her.'

'Yes — but when he telephoned the marchesa, Mrs Spenser hadn't arrived. Apparently her daughter received a telegram to say that she had decided to stay in Paris for a few days and would join the family later.'

'That's all right, then. What's the problem?'

'It's not all right. Wagstaff rang the hotel in Paris where she usually stays, but she wasn't there. They hadn't seen her, or even heard from her, for more than a year. Wagstaff wondered if she'd written to me, but of course she hadn't. It's worrying — it's most unlike her to go off like that without letting anyone know.'

'She could be tired of people keeping tabs on her,' suggested Valerie. 'Like I am!'

'Oh, no,' said Toby. 'Unlike you, Mrs Spenser is a very straightforward person, with nothing to hide.'

'What do you mean by that?'

'Simply that you're not particularly straightforward, Mrs Markham. Are you quite sure you haven't heard from her?'

'I've already said we haven't. Why should I lie about it?'

'You might. After all, you are a professional liar, aren't you?'

'What do you mean?'

He laughed: 'Of course, I'm testing you,' he said. 'But you haven't been altogether truthful, have you? There are some things about you I didn't know. And I'm sure Mrs Spenser didn't know them either.'

Valerie tried to stifle the panic his words had roused in her. How could he possibly have discovered her secret? But, if he had found out that she was not the woman to whom his friend had let her house, what could he really do about it? She must keep her temper.

'When I wanted to know why you hadn't gone to Brazil with your husband, you told me that you had to stay and look after the children. Now it turns out that you are a professional actress. So who looks after them when you're away from home, acting?'

'They go to boarding-school.'

'Of course. But why did you tell Mrs Spenser that you were a straightforward, happily-married young mum who was perfectly content to stay at home and look after her family?'

'Did I?'

'You must have done! Otherwise she would never have accepted you as a suitable tenant!'

'Why ever not? I assure you, Mr Anderson, that I am a very responsible person. Certainly not a rogue or a vagabond.'

'Even if you do earn your living by telling lies?'

'And what exactly do you mean by that?'

'As I told you, I know very little about your profession. But, so far as I'm concerned, trying to convince other people that you are not the person they know you to be but someone completely different — isn't that simply telling lies? When you say you're Juliet, or Lady Macbeth, or the Widow Twankey, you expect them to believe you . . .'

'Of course: while they're watching the play.'

'Then you're telling lies.'

'No — I'm telling the truth. When I am on stage, then I *am* Juliet, or Lady Macbeth. I've never played the Widow Twankey . . .'

He ignored her joke. 'But it's still telling lies! You're really Ms Markham, no matter how you look or what you say.'

'It's the truth. Perhaps another sort of truth . . .'

'There's only one sort of truth,' said Toby. 'Perhaps I'm just a simple countryman, but I can recognize a lie when I hear it. Why, you're not even a proper mother! I've never heard your daughter call you anything but 'Val'. I know that's the modern way, but I should have thought that any normal young woman would be glad to have a lovely little girl like Lisa call her 'Mummy'. I'm disappointed in you — and so would Mrs Spenser be. She'd be very angry if she found out what you do for a living.'

'But that's ridiculous!' said Valerie, 'and, in any case, you have no right to speak to me in that way.'

'No right at all,' he agreed, 'I'm sorry.' Of course, he did not sound at all sorry although, all the time he was speaking to her, Valerie thought she saw a look in his eyes which belied the harshness of his words — almost as if he were pleading with her to tell him that he was completely mistaken about her. Imagination! she told herself. Just because she found him attractive, there was no earthly reason for him to like her, or even approve of her. At least, she should be thankful that he still believed that she was Lisa's mother — and married to Alex.

'I'm sorry if you think I'm speaking out of turn,' he said, 'but I am really concerned about Mrs Spenser. Wagstaff and I are both worried that something may have happened to her.'

'I'm sure everything's all right,' said Valerie. 'She's bound to turn up at her daughter's house in a day or two.'

'I hope so.'

* * *

Next day, two letters arrived for Valerie. She assumed that they had come through the post, though it was actually Toby who handed them to her.

'I met Harold down the road,' he said casually, 'so, as I'm coming this way, I offered to save him a journey.'

Valerie flushed: so now, it seemed, he was checking her mail! She managed to hide her anger and took the letters from him with a smile. Both of them were from Brazil: one was addressed to Mrs Markham and the other to Ms V

Markham, and both were typed. Toby glanced at her curiously as she slipped them into her pocket. She caught his eye and felt herself blushing as she asked him, 'Were you coming to see me?'

'Yes. I wanted to apologize to you for the way I spoke to you yesterday. I have to go to Oakham on business this afternoon. I wondered if the children would like to come with me. They might be interested in the Rutland Museum and the castle. I expect they're tired of staying round the house all the time — and it would give you a break, too.'

'That's a kind thought,' she said. 'Thank you very much. Of course, Richard might be tied up with his friend Colin and the ferrets, but I'll ask him.'

'Then perhaps I could take Lisa? I already have a passenger — the lady clerk from the forest office is coming with me — her mother's not well and she wants to go and see her.'

'Well, then, if Lisa would like to go . . . '

'Actually it was her own idea,' said Toby.

'Do you mean that she asked you? When?'

'I met her early this morning, up near East Lodge.'

'East Lodge?'

'Do you remember that evening when you saw those three deer? There used to be another farmhouse there — it burned down about fifty years ago. You probably saw those piles of rubble . . . '

'Lisa had no business to go up there by herself! She knows she's not supposed to wander about on her own. Ever since Mrs Gregory . . . '

'I brought her back,' said Toby. 'I was quite sure you wouldn't allow her to go out by herself. She didn't want me to tell you, but of course it's only right you should know.'

'What was she doing?'

'She said she was looking for deer.

Please don't be too cross with her, Ms Markham. It must be very dull to be kept in all the time when there are so many interesting things to see in the forest.'

'Yes. What time are you leaving for Oakham?'

'About one o'clock. If the children would like to meet me outside the office . . . '

Valerie did not open her mail until the children had gone to meet Toby. She looked at the two envelopes. One must be from Alex and the other from Vanessa. Alex's letter was probably not for her at all but it was impossible to tell which was which, because the postmarks were so badly smudged that they were undecipherable.

Thinking that the one addressed to Ms V Markham was the more likely to be from Vanessa, she opened it first. Written from a hotel in Rio, it told her that Alex had already left for a small town up the Amazon, which was to be his base for the next few weeks, and that Vanessa intended to join him there. She did not say a lot, simply hoping that the children were behaving themselves and that Valerie was able to cope with the rather awkward situation in which she had placed her.

'You can say that again!' said Valerie aloud. She would certainly tell Vanessa exactly what she thought of her, when she appeared at Greenleafe!

She hesitated before opening the other letter. After all, it was not intended for her but for her sister. Alex must have written it before he received Vanessa's telegram, when he had no idea of her intention to join him. However, realizing that it probably contained messages for Lisa and Richard, she knew that she must have some idea of what he had said.

The envelope did contain separate notes for each of the children: she would hand them over as soon as they returned from their outing. She wondered if she should have allowed them to go. After all, Toby was a stranger, about whom she knew very little. But of course, she told herself, he was on friendly terms with the foresters and the trusty Mr Bagster — not to mention the police! Several times she had seen him chatting, not only to Sergeant Weeks but to the C.I.D. officers who were investigating the murder.

Should she, or should she not, read Alex's letter to Vanessa? What decided her was knowing that, were their positions reversed, her sister would have had no qualms at all about reading a letter addressed to her! So she gave in to her curiosity.

She had taken one of the white painted garden chairs on to the lawn between the herbaceous borders. It was a warm, bright afternoon, throbbing with the hum of bees. Only the occasional shriek of a distant chain saw reminded her that other people were at work. Hilda had gone home after lunch and, for once, there was no sign of Mr Bagster anywhere in the garden. Valerie sighed — it was blissful to have this lovely place to herself, for once!

Obviously written before he knew of Vanessa's decision to join him, Valerie wondered why this letter had taken such a long time to arrive. Perhaps, knowing what Alex was like when he was concentrating on his work, he had carried it about for some time before he remembered to post it! Much of it was concerned with the hotel where he was staying while he completed the preparations for his trip. She read this part with amusement and, to tell the truth, not a little envy. She knew that she would have been far more use to him on such an expedition than her scatter-brained sister. Alex should have married her, not Vanessa. But perish the thought! He was the last man in the world she would ever have wanted to marry.

The next sentences surprised her. 'I am so thankful,' Alex had written, 'that you took my advice and decided against coming on this expedition. Although one can be immunized against most diseases, there are many other hazards of a different kind, against which it is almost impossible to guard oneself. I would not want you to be exposed to them, my darling. My own time will be fully occupied looking after my own safety, without the added responsibility of guarding you against dangers of which you have no conception.

'Please don't think I'm being arrogant or selfish — much as I would love to have you with me, I know that your place is with the children. If anything happened to me, they would need your love and care. Not that I anticipate disaster: I look forward to joining you in this wonderful house you have found for us.

'I think about you most of the time, my dearest love . . .'

At this point, Valerie put the letter away. She had no right to pry into the intimacy between a man and his wife, even though his wife was so close to her that she seemed almost part of herself.

Sighing, she replaced the letter in its

envelope. How she wished that it had arrived before Vanessa's departure. It was not unlikely, of course, that her sister would have ignored its warning and carried out her plan to surprise Alex with her sudden arrival in Brazil, but there was at least a chance that she might have seen sense.

Recalling the disturbing dreams she had had about Vanessa, Valerie was suddenly frightened. Suppose that something terrible did happen to them? Who would look after the children then? Richard's mother's parents were still alive and she knew that he had uncles and aunts, but Lisa had nobody — nobody except herself. And she was a not-all-that-successful actress who sometimes found it as much as she could do to keep her own head above water.

'Nonsense!' she said to herself. 'Nothing's going to happen to Vanessa or Alex!' Prophetic dreams, she told herself, are a load of nonsense — just like Lisa's childish fears of walking skeletons. Nevertheless, a shadow had dimmed the sunshine of her perfect afternoon.

'Valerie!' She looked round to see who had spoken. It was Peter, looking pleased with himself, his blond hair glinting in the sunshine. He really was incredibly handsome, she thought. Now, instead of that scruffy anorak, he was wearing a smart linen jacket, with a silk scarf knotted round his neck, and expensive looking leather sandals.

'All alone?' he asked affably. 'How did you manage to get rid of the children? You look deliciously cool in that cotton frock.'

'Where have you sprung from?'

'I thought I'd pay you a visit. Nobody answered the front door bell, so I decided to walk round the garden and see if you were at home. And here you are.'

'I thought you'd gone back to London.'

'So I had. When the garage got round to repairing my car, I decided to take the things I'd picked up at those sales back to my shop.'

'Did you find anything interesting?'

'Not a lot. Most saleable items seem to have found their way to America already. It's an expensive business, replacing stock. But I decided not to stay in London: I left my assistant in charge and came back here — like a moth to a candle flame!'

'It's a very attractive place, certainly,' agreed Valerie, 'though I should hardly expect it to lure you away from the bright lights.'

'What about yourself?' he countered. 'I don't think you're much of a country mouse, either. I find your conversion to rural domesticity very surprising. Or perhaps you didn't have much choice?'

'What do you mean by that?'

'Nothing in particular. Of course, there are reasons why a talented young actress might decide to get married and raise a family, but I didn't think that was the path you would have chosen, my dear. But apparently I was wrong.'

His manner changed abruptly.

'You don't look at all pleased to see me,' he said.

'Don't I?'

'No — considering what great friends we used to be in the old days.'

'Everybody in that company was friendly,' said Valerie, 'but of course, I haven't seen any of them for ages. You know what it's like; when you're working with people in the theatre, you get very close. But afterwards, you tend to forget about them. Rather like the other patients one meets in hospital.'

'I wouldn't know,' said Peter stiffly, 'I've never been in hospital. But I really did think you'd be a lot more pleased to see me again.'

'Of course I'm pleased!' Valerie was puzzled. She had very clear memories of the summer they had spent at that holiday camp. They had performed in a series of plays — three cut-down versions of recent West End successes — put on to entertain the campers. Once they had finished rehearsing all three plays, they performed them in rotation, a week at a time, throughout the season. Once they were running, the company had most days to themselves, free to enjoy the amenities of the camp or to explore the nearby town, just as their fancy led them. She did not remember spending much time with Peter, much as she would have liked to. He had been dancing attendance on one of the older actresses — the leading lady, as a matter of fact — and he had made it clear that Valerie, who had only just left drama school, did not interest him at all. She was surprised that he even remembered who she was.

As he chatted about the beauties of Greenleafe and admired the well kept garden, she remembered some more things about him and wondered why it was that she had had such a crush on him. Although he was a competent actor who, at times, gave a performance which was not far short of brilliant, he was very undisciplined. Even Valerie had had to admit that he was conceited. And mean — not only with money, but in his attitude to the rest of the company. In every scene in which he appeared, he contrived to take the centre of the stage.

She realized that he had stopped babbling about the beauties of nature and had now begun to ask questions.

'Where did you meet Alex?' he asked.

'I didn't. We'd always known each other. He's my cousin.'

'So you decided to marry him,' Peter sighed. 'What a fool I was! I should have told you at the time how I felt about you!'

'I thought you did — at least, I got the message. You and Nina Dawn were completely inseparable that summer. You made it quite clear that you had no time for me, or anybody else.'

'I may have given that impression,' Peter assured her, 'but it was just a big cover-up. You were a most disturbing young lady, Valerie. And you still are.'

'Don't be ridiculous!'

'Ridiculous?' he repeated. 'I was at that time — how long ago was it? But I've got over it now. I'm not so shy as I used to be.'

'You were never shy. Still, as you said, it's a long time ago and things are quite different now. I think I'd better go indoors and start getting the children's tea.'

'Children!' he snorted. 'It shocks me to see you so weighed down by domesticity! A free spirit like you, with a wonderful career ahead of you, to be stuck with a boring husband who leaves you holding the fort while he charges off to foreign parts! You're worth so much more than that, darling.'

'I haven't given up my career,' she said, 'and your pity is completely wasted on me. So now, if you'll excuse me . . . '

'Why not invite me in for a cup of tea?'

'Another time, perhaps, when I'm not so busy.'

'How can you be so unkind? You're

not afraid of me, are you? There's no need to be. I'd never do anything to hurt you, my dear.'

He put his arms round her and gazed into her eyes. His own, she realized, were very pale blue — so pale that they were almost colourless. His lips hovered close to hers. How strange it was that, at one time, she would have been thrilled by the prospect of being kissed by this man. Thrilled and flattered. Now the idea revolted her. She wriggled free, muttering, 'Don't be so silly!'

'What's silly about wanting to kiss you? Just because you're married to that lump of a man . . . '

'Alex isn't a lump.'

'Don't tell me that you're in love with him.'

Valerie felt herself blushing: what could she possibly say?

'I'm surprised that you're so conventional,' sneered Peter. 'What's the harm? I doubt if Alex would grudge you a bit of fun. After all, he's on the other side of the Atlantic — no doubt having it off with some dark-eyed *señorita* . . .'

'I think you'd better go,' said Valerie, tight-lipped.

'I'm very disappointed in you,' he said.

They heard a car approaching. It stopped, apparently outside the front gate.

'I'll see you again,' said Peter. He walked quickly away from the house, in the direction of the vegetable garden.

Valerie walked round the house and met Toby and the children, just as they arrived at the front door.

'You're back early,' she said. 'Is everything all right?'

'Lisa started to feel sick,' said Richard disgustedly, 'so we came back.'

'It wasn't my fault,' protested Lisa.

'Are you all right?' Toby was not looking at Lisa but at Valerie. 'Has something upset you?'

'Of course not,' Valerie dismissed the idea. 'What about Lisa?'

'I'm all right, Val. I wasn't really sick. Just wobbly.'

'Never mind,' said Toby, 'we'll go and have a look at the museum another time. And I'll take plenty of barley sugar with me, just in case! Perhaps you'd like to come with us next time, Ms Markham?'

'I should like that,' said Valerie politely.

'Guess who we saw in Oakham,' said Lisa, 'Mr Bagster! I didn't recognize him at first — he wasn't wearing his overalls. He was with Mrs Bagster. She said she had to go to some special shop.'

'He said I was to apologize,' said Richard, 'and that he'll come in this evening to look at the boiler.'

'He had no business to go off like that,' protested Toby. 'He was supposed to be working here this afternoon. At least he should have told you he wasn't coming.'

'It really doesn't matter.' Valerie wondered why Toby seemed so upset. Was it only because Lisa had felt sick that he had come hurrying back to

Greenleafe? Perhaps she was getting paranoid — it was unlikely that Mr Bagster's defection should have made all that difference. It had been so delightful to be on her own, for once — at least, until Peter's unexpected arrival.

Toby refused her offer of tea, saying that he had to go out again shortly. However, when the children went indoors, he asked her to walk down to the gate with him.

'Are you sure nothing's the matter, Mrs Markham? You looked quite worried when we arrived.'

'I was simply surprised that you came back so soon.'

'I thought it might be something more than that.'

'Look here!' said Valerie crossly, 'It's enough to make anyone worried, the way you people fuss over me. I am a grown woman, you know, not a silly schoolgirl. I am used to being on my own and I'm not in the least frightened. It was a pleasure to have the place to myself, for once.'

'Sorry!' said Toby. 'Obviously, I'm intruding.'

'And I'm sorry Lisa spoilt your afternoon. I should have warned you that she has these occasional bouts of car sickness.'

'It wasn't as bad as all that — it was just that I was afraid she might start feeling worse.'

Now Valerie felt really angry. 'Are you sure that is why you decided to come back? It wasn't by any chance because you saw Mr Bagster and realized that he had deserted his post and that there was nobody to keep an eye on me this afternoon?'

'Why ever should you think that?'

'Because you're making it so obvious. Do I have to keep telling you that I've no intention of running away with Mrs Spenser's silver teapot? That I'm not going to burn the house down if I'm left alone for more than a few minutes? Isn't there something in the lease about 'quiet enjoyment'? Surely I'm entitled to enjoy living here quietly, without Mrs Spenser's friends and employees dogging my steps. I can scarcely move without one or other of you suddenly popping up! Does somebody patrol the house at night, too? With a bull's-eye lamp? That wouldn't surprise me.'

'There's no need to be paranoid,' said Toby.

'Isn't there?'

Afterwards, Valerie had to admit to herself that she knew why she was so angry. She was now almost convinced that she was being watched — and, of course, she did have something to hide. But why did Mrs Spenser think it so important that the house should never be left unattended? Had she some pathological fear of burglars? The place was very nicely furnished, of course, but there was nothing in it to attract professional art thieves. There were no valuable antiques, original oil paintings, or anything like that. There was no expensive hi-fi equipment and the very ordinary little television set was certainly not in its first youth!

What about the locked room? Mrs Gregory had mentioned knick-knacks and curios, but she had made it quite clear that Mrs Spenser had deposited her valuable jewellery in the bank. So why all this cloak and dagger secrecy?

'Old people do sometimes get cranky,' she tried to reassure herself, but it was no good. The whole set up, not to mention her own tender conscience about something she no longer regarded as a harmless charade, had set her nerves on edge.

Where did Peter fit in? Was he, too, part of the arrangement to keep her under observation? Unlikely — he was, no doubt, exactly what he claimed to be; a Londoner. He had, like herself, fallen under the spell of this part of the country, which was so much further off the beaten track than the places most favoured by tourists — the West Country, for instance, or the Lake District.

Apart from weekends, when parties

of trippers drove over to Greenleafe from places like Peterborough or Kettering to spend a quiet afternoon wandering in woods, the forest was fairly free from visitors, even at the height of summer. Had it not been for the irritation of being kept under watch — and, of course, for the robbery and death of poor Mrs Gregory — Valerie would have been perfectly happy living at West Lodge.

6

Next day was Friday. As soon as Hilda had arrived at West Lodge, Valerie and the children set out for Stirbridge. She had had another disturbed night, the only dreams she could remember being about Vanessa and some danger which threatened her, and she was not in a good temper. She was quite sharp with poor Lisa, who was still trying to persuade her to have a birthday party and was not at all interested in going for a picnic at Rutland Water instead.

'Grown-ups don't celebrate birthdays,' said Valerie firmly.

'Mummy always does,' Lisa assured her, 'and this year, it's a special one, isn't it? You'll be thirty.'

This was something of which Valerie would prefer not to be reminded. Already thirty years old — and she was neither married nor established in a successful career. Nor was there any immediate prospect either of romance or of stardom.

She suddenly thought about Peter. He had given up and, to judge by his clothes and well-groomed appearance the day before, the antiques business was a better proposition than his acting career had ever been. She had been very surprised by his sudden interest in herself, which was the last thing she would have expected or wanted. Years ago, she had certainly found him attractive and, had he shown any interest in her while they were working at the holiday camp, who knew what might have happened? But he had ignored her and she soon realized that his good looks were really all he had going for him.

Now the silly man was trying to persuade her that he had been interested in her all along! Why? She knew it wasn't true. Of course, it was probably just because he thought that she might be available — a temporarily deserted wife might be glad of a diversion to relieve the monotony of her grass-widowhood!

As usual on market day, Stirbridge was crowded. She managed to find a place in one of the car-parks, not too far from the town centre, and then made her way to Broad Street to visit her bank. Richard and Lisa had shopping of their own to do, so she left them to their own devices, telling them to meet her outside the public library at twelve o'clock.

Her business at the bank did not take long, so she had plenty of time to do the necessary shopping. She carried her purchases back to the car-park and then went window-shopping. It surprised her that such a small town should boast such a variety of good shops. She was looking in the window of a draper's shop at an attractive display of dress materials and trying to remember if she had seen a sewing machine in one of the spare bedrooms, when a deep voice beside her made her turn and look up into the dark eyes of Toby Anderson.

'Don't look so startled!' he said, with a laugh, 'I'm not following you about. Honest! Most people come to Stir-bridge on a Friday, so one is quite likely to see everyone one knows.'

'Of course.' Valerie shelved the idea of making herself a summer frock and smiled up at him.

'That's better,' he said. 'For once you don't look worried. What have you done with the children? Left them at Greenleafe?'

'No. They want to do some shopping of their own, so I'm meeting them later.'

'Have you time for a cup of coffee?' he asked. 'I'm just about ready for one.'

Why not? She looked at her watch, saw that she had nearly an hour to spare before she had to meet the children and accepted his invitation.

The Honeysuckle Tea Rooms were at the far end of one of the narrow alleys leading from the High Street to the embankment which overlooked the town meadows. Toby took her to a table near the window, from which they could see across the meadows to where the River Stir meandered gently behind a screen of willows.

'This is a beautiful place,' she said. 'How lovely to find this open space, right in the middle of the town.'

'Of course,' said Toby, 'that low-lying land tends to get flooded. Otherwise there's no doubt that someone would have built on it long ago.'

'Does it often get flooded?'

'Oh yes, particularly in the winter. Then, when there's a heavy frost, the whole of the meadows get frozen over. It makes a wonderful skating rink! They say that, years ago, it was possible to skate right down the river to where it joins the Welland and beyond, right down as far as Boston. But we don't have frosts like that nowadays.'

' 'Where are the snows of yester-year?' ' Valerie quoted, laughing.

'Where indeed, Ms Markham. But I

didn't ask you here to talk about the weather.'

'What then? Do I gather that you have something to tell me?'

'Yes. Did you know that the police have let old Jim go?'

'No — I hadn't heard. Oh, dear . . . '

'Why, what's the matter? Of course, you never saw Jim, or you'd realize that he couldn't possibly have attacked Dora Gregory. I was very relieved that he could prove he was nowhere near Greenleafe when it happened.'

'No, I don't know the man. I had no idea that the police had got hold of the wrong person. I wish they hadn't — it means that whoever did kill her is still at large, and I shall have to go on keeping those poor children at home. They will be very disappointed.'

'Better to be disappointed than to risk running into danger. Whoever was responsible may still be in the district. If either of the children was in the forest that morning, they could easily have seen something, or somebody . . . '

'I'm sure they didn't. They would have told me if they'd seen anything suspicious,' said Valerie.

'If they had realized at the time that what they saw had any significance,' said Toby. 'I thought I'd tell you that the police will probably want to ask them some more questions. And, if that happens, somebody else might want to make sure that they give the right answers — or don't answer at all.'

'Whatever do you mean?'

'I don't want to alarm you, Ms Markham. But Please, please don't allow the children to wander about by themselves. Particularly Lisa.'

'Aren't you being melodramatic?' asked Valerie. 'Isn't it obvious that whoever knocked that poor old lady on the head was simply after her money? He will be miles away by now. I don't suppose your friend Jim is the only vagrant in the district. I have no intention of allowing Lisa to go out by herself but really — I do think you're making rather a meal of all this.'

'I wonder,' said Toby. 'But, Ms Markham, if I can help in any way, you only have to ask. I'd be glad to take Richard and Lisa out sometimes. You too, if you like. There are lots of interesting places to visit round here . . .'

'It's very kind of you, Mr Anderson, but surely you have your work to do?'

'Of course — but I do think this is something of an emergency. Until the police have a definite lead, taking care of your children is a priority.'

'I'm surprised you should look at it in that way.'

'Are you?' His brown eyes held hers in that disturbing way, as if he were saying far less than he intended, or wanted, to tell her. She thought she had better change the subject.

'Do you know if Mr Wagstaff has been able to contact Mrs Spenser?'

'No, he hasn't. So far, there's been no sign of her. He's getting really worried.'

It had been a mistake to mention Mrs Spenser. It was, Valerie thought, completely ridiculous that these people seemed to get so worked up over trifles! But it was as if Toby had read her mind.

'Mrs Spenser's an old lady,' he explained gently. 'She doesn't look it, but she's well over seventy. How old did you think she was?'

An embarrassing question because, of course, Valerie had never met the woman. It was Vanessa who had been given tea at West Lodge when the tenancy was being discussed.

'I had no idea,' she said truthfully.

'I should have thought you would be a good judge of ages,' he chided her. 'As an actress, aren't you a student of such things? But, whatever you thought, she's nearly seventy-eight. Ladies of that age don't usually go walk-about without telling somebody what they're doing, or where they're going.'

'She may have told Mrs Gregory,' suggested Valerie, but she realized as soon as she spoke that this could not have been the case. Mrs Gregory had given no indication that her employer intended to go anywhere except to her daughter's home in Italy.

She looked at her watch. 'Heavens! Is that the time? I must get to the library — I'm meeting the children in five minutes.'

'It isn't far,' he reassured her, calling the waitress and paying the bill. Outside the café, he took his leave of her.

'Don't forget what I said. I'll be glad to help with the children. And if I can do anything else for you, please don't hesitate to ask. My caravan's outside the barn in the Commission's yard — go through the barn and out of the door the other side. I'm there most evenings.'

She thanked him and hurried up the alley towards the library, where the children were already waiting for her. Richard was holding an oblong parcel which looked like a book. Whatever Lisa had bought was obviously small enough to go into her pocket.

'Finished your shopping?' asked Valerie.

'Ages ago!' replied Lisa. 'Where have you been?'

'I met Mr Anderson and we had coffee together.'

'That's nice!' said Lisa. 'We went into a café too. I had a chocolate ice-cream. Would you like a jelly baby?' She took a paper bag out of her pocket and offered it. Valerie took a sweet and her heart gave a little leap: it seemed such a little while ago that she and Vanessa had spent their pocket money on such delights. Jelly babies had been one of her own favourites — particularly the pink ones. Toby's words came back to her, recalling the idea that Lisa, her lovely little Lisa, might have run unwittingly into some danger. It was an appalling idea — but surely he was wrong? What could Lisa possibly have seen that morning which would interest the police, or anyone else? Should she ask the child? No: that would only make things worse. With the resilience of youth, Lisa seemed to have forgotten all about Mrs Gregory and what had happened to her, so it would be better to let the matter rest.

All the way home, Lisa was in a fever of excitement. Valerie guessed that she had been buying something for her birthday and she knew very well what the child was feeling. She was longing to show her her present straight away, although she was determined to keep it as a surprise! She remembered similar conflicts when she was a child: she was pleased when Lisa did not yield to temptation but took her purchase upstairs to her room without giving the game away.

Richard had no such problems. It was no hardship to him to put his parcel away until the proper time. Stolid, unimaginative — just like his father.

Although she had protested when Peter called Alex 'a lump', she had often wondered what Vanessa saw in him. But, of course, Alex was a scientist, not an artist. He dealt only with facts. The 'other sort of truth' of which she had spoken to Toby meant nothing to Alex at all. She wondered how he had reacted when Vanessa told him how they were deceiving Mrs Spenser and her friends. No doubt he would disapprove!

Valerie was finding it surprisingly difficult to play mother to her sister's children. For Richard, of course, there was no problem. She doubted if he had ever really accepted Vanessa as a substitute for his real mother. But with Lisa it was quite different. Close as she felt to the little girl, she could not guess what she really thought about their relationship. Lisa seemed happy enough, apart from the restrictions imposed on her since Mrs Gregory's death — but how happy was she really? Valerie was half afraid that Lisa might believe her real mother had rejected her.

After lunch, the children set up the clock golf course in the garden. Hilda had gone home but Mr Bagster was in attendance, apparently tidying up his potting shed, though she was fairly certain that his real function was doing his turn of guard duty. For once, Valerie was not so much annoyed by the surveillance as amused by it.

She was in the study writing letters when someone banged on the front door. Not expecting any visitors, she was surprised to find Mr Wagstaff waiting on the step.

'I should have let you know I was coming,' he said, 'but I only decided this morning, when there was no point in trying to phone you. I expect you went to Stirbridge market. I hope I haven't called at an inconvenient time?'

'Not at all.' She invited him in and went into the kitchen to make tea. The children were still playing golf, so she left them where they were while she found out the purpose of the solicitor's visit.

'How are you getting on with Hilda? I hope her work is satisfactory, Mrs Markham.'

'She's splendid. I'm thankful she has

a car. After what happened, I shouldn't like the thought of her cycling or walking through the forest. It would worry me, even if I thought the police had arrested somebody.'

'Have you heard that they haven't charged Jim Barley?' asked Mr Wagstaff.

She nodded. 'So it's back to square one.'

'Quite so. But I wanted to talk to you about something else, Mrs Markham. I expect you know that I've been trying to get in touch with Mrs Spenser.'

'Hasn't she arrived at her daughter's home yet?'

'I'm afraid not: she seems to have vanished. Both the marchesa and I are very concerned about her. She's an old lady, Mrs Markham, and her heart is none too good. The last time anyone actually spoke to her was when she went to her bank in Stirbridge, just before you came here. She handed over a box for safe keeping, but did not wait to see the manager.'

'Why should she have seen him?' asked Valerie.

'This is a small community. He's not only her bank manager, but a personal friend. As I am. He was a little surprised that she didn't say goodbye to him. When I spoke to him a few days ago, he told me that she hadn't collected the foreign currency and travellers cheques she'd ordered.'

'That's odd,' said Valerie, 'I should have thought that she would have dealt with that when she deposited her jewellery.'

'Exactly: it is most curious. The reason I'm telling you this is so that you will understand why the marchesa wants to come to the house. Of course, she is Mrs Spenser's next of kin.'

'Isn't there a son too?' asked Valerie. 'Mrs Gregory was telling us about him . . .'

'Simon Spenser is not concerned with this,' said Mr Wagstaff. 'His mother would not wish him to be involved. Of course, that's a family matter. To come straight to the point, I shall be bringing the marchesa here on Sunday. I believe Mrs Gregory had a key to Mrs Spenser's room, though we weren't able to find it among her belongings.'

'She didn't carry it about with her,' said Valerie. 'She kept it here. I know where it is.'

'Good. Then we won't have to force the lock. You see, Mrs Markham, she may have left a note for Mrs Gregory, to tell her about any last-minute change of plan.'

'I'll get the key,' said Valerie, 'if you want to look now.'

'No,' he said. 'Best wait until Angela arrives.'

'Angela?'

'The marchesa. She wants to be present when I open the door.'

'And she's coming on Sunday?'

'I'm afraid so. I'm sorry to disturb you at the weekend — but we're all very concerned. I do hope it won't be too inconvenient.'

'Of course not!'

'Then we'll be here soon after lunch,' said Mr Wagstaff.

7

'Looking forward to your birthday, Val?' asked Lisa next morning.

'Not a lot,' said Valerie.

'Why can't we have a party? It's so dull here, now that you won't let us go in the forest.'

'Cheer up, sweetheart. It won't be all that long before your mummy and daddy come back. Then we can have a party to celebrate.'

'Oh, Val — it's weeks and weeks. And then we shall be going to school. Why did we have to leave Yorkshire? When we lived there, I had lots of other girls to play with. And I could ride the pony. Now you won't even let me ride that bicycle. And I did so want to explore the rest of the forest.'

'Perhaps you can, in a week or two,' said Valerie vaguely. Lisa sighed; then she thought of something else.

'Are you wondering what I'm going to give you for your birthday present?' she asked. 'I bet you'd never guess what it is.'

'I expect I shall have to wait and see.'

'Do you know what Richard's giving you?'

'Well, I think he bought a book yesterday. But he hasn't said anything.'

'I expect he wants it to be a surprise, too. I do hope you'll like my present — I think it's beautiful.'

'I'm sure I shall like it, dear.'

Valerie, for some reason, was dreading the marchesa's visit. She had had another restless night, during which her dreams about Vanessa, although she could not remember the details, had included Mr Wagstaff and his clients. She felt drawn and headachy and, when Mr Bagster came to look at the boiler, even he noticed that something was wrong.

'Is anything the matter, Mrs Markham?'

'Nothing really, thank you. I didn't

sleep too well — there was quite a wind, and you know how old houses sometimes creak and groan.'

'As long as that's all. I don't want to alarm you, but there are some odd people about. You are careful to lock and bolt all the doors before you go to bed, aren't you?'

'Yes, of course I am. Except the door from the small sitting-room into the conservatory, of course. That hasn't a bolt. But it's always locked last thing at night.'

'Then I think I should fit a bolt. One can't be too careful. I shall be going into town this afternoon, so I'll call at the ironmonger's and get one. I'll fit it as soon as I get back. You will be in, won't you, Mrs Markham?'

'I'm not planning to go anywhere today. I might take Lisa for a walk, but I shan't go far.'

'That's all right, then. Expect me about five o'clock.'

Why the panic? Why had he come into the open, more or less admitting that it was he who was responsible for the security of West Lodge? At least it no longer seemed that she was the cause of all their doubts and misgivings. That, at least, was something to be thankful for.

Lisa didn't want to go for a walk that afternoon. She had been whispering to Richard most of the morning, obviously trying to get him to do some little job for her.

'You said you could do it yourself,' he grumbled. 'Can't you see I'm trying to read this book?'

'I'm afraid I can't manage it after all.'

Richard sighed and closed his book. 'All right, nuisance! I'll get a pair of pliers.'

They were still bickering when Valerie went out: even if Lisa didn't want to come with her, she would enjoy a short walk. She strolled past the green and along the road between the wood and the green tunnels, not intending to go very far because, after what Mr Bagster had said that morning, she did not want to leave the children on their own for very long.

No wonder Lisa was getting bored! Although there were plenty of things in the attic to play with, it couldn't be much fun by herself. Richard, of course, considered that he had far better things to do than to entertain his little sister. In any case, much of his time was spent with Colin and the ferrets.

Valerie herself was very disappointed with the way things had turned out. The house was even more delightful than Vanessa had led her to believe — she sometimes dreamed about living there permanently. If only her career had brought her a lot of money! She would have tried to persuade Mrs Spenser to sell West Lodge to her. Apart from the house, Valerie had come to like the forest, too. And she had no complaints about the children: they were behaving very well. Yet, instead of a holiday to which she had been looking forward, Valerie felt almost as if she were under house arrest!

Soon, without realizing that she had walked so far, she reached the end of the road. Before her lay the apparently empty field, where she had spotted those deer, and the mounds of rubble which she now knew were the remains of East Lodge. She wondered who had once lived there and what the house had been like before the fire. She doubted if there were anyone now living at Greenleafe, or even in Petercliffe, who could remember it.

A movement among the fern caught her eye. Some animal or bird, no doubt, which had made its home among the ruins. Cautiously, she made her way towards the mound. Then, to her surprise, Peter suddenly stood up and walked towards her.

'Hello!' she said. 'What are you doing here?'

'I might ask you the same thing. I guess that, like me, you're just out for a walk.'

'That's right. Is there anything

interesting among those ruins?'

'What, for instance?'

'Birds' nests. Fox holes. Rabbit burrows.'

'No, nothing like that. I don't really know why I bothered to look,' he said. 'Where are you walking to?'

'Nowhere in particular. In fact, I'm just about to turn back. It will soon be time to get the children's tea.'

'Oh, your never-ending chore. You should train them to get their own tea, my dear. Shall I walk back with you?'

'You can if you like.' She had not intended to sound quite so ungracious but, to tell the truth, she did not welcome his company at that moment. Or anyone else's, she told herself firmly.

'Still fascinated by this place?' she asked after a moment or two.

'Yes. Any reason why I shouldn't be?'

'Things have changed since Mrs Gregory died. Poor Lisa's getting so bored — I don't want to alarm her but obviously I can't let her wander about on her own.'

'Surely there's no danger?' he asked. 'Whoever attacked the old woman will be miles away by now. He surely wouldn't hang about here when he realized the police were still looking for him.'

'Don't they say that a criminal always returns to the scene of the crime?'

'Surely that's just an old wives' tale.'

'Perhaps. But the people round here seem to think I should go on being careful.'

'That's what I mean. They're only a bunch of country bumpkins, after all. And if you do believe them, should you be walking about by yourself?'

'I'm surely better able to take care of myself than Lisa.'

'Why should she be in any particular danger?'

'She went for a walk the morning before the murder. She could have seen something — something which nobody thought was suspicious at the time. Now the police have let that tramp go, they might want to ask her a lot more questions.'

'Isn't that rather far-fetched? Surely you're worrying yourself unduly.' He sighed, 'I find it very odd that you've become such a mother hen. You were such a sexy little piece when we were at that holiday camp — it's incredible that you should have changed so much.'

'Was I? Really, Peter — when we were at Valmouth, we hardly knew each other. Your memory must be playing you tricks.'

'I don't think so. I may not have had as much to do with you as I should have liked, but that was because I was naturally cautious. How old were you? Nineteen? A nineteen-year-old virgin would have been far too dangerous to get entangled with. But now . . .'

'Now I have other commitments,' she said.

'But you admit that you're bored. I can be very entertaining company you know, my darling Valerie.'

'I'm sure you can! Thank you, Peter, but I think the children give me all the entertainment I need.'

'You could invite me to tea one afternoon, when the children are out. Or to coffee, when they're in bed. I'm sure we could pass the time together very pleasantly. Why not indulge in a little light relaxation?'

'Don't be so stupid,' she snapped. 'It's not on, and you know it!'

'Well, I shall probably be here for a few days longer, in case you change your mind.' He was not at all abashed.

They were approaching the turn off to Petercliffe when she caught sight of a tall figure striding towards them past the green tunnels. She did not know if Peter had seen him but, when they reached the road junction, he turned to her, saying, 'Since you haven't invited me to tea, I'd better go back to the village and see if my landlady will give me any. Goodbye, Valerie. I hope we're still friends.'

'Of course!' she said lightly. 'As long as you remember that this isn't Valmouth.'

'You're obviously not going to let me forget that,' he said, turning briskly down the side road.

Walking to meet Toby, she had the feeling that he was coming to look for her. For once she was glad: she did not feel at all comfortable in Peter's presence, although she was fairly certain that his advances were mostly banter. Toby's presence was, she felt, no kind of threat and she was quite pleased when, after greeting her, he turned and walked back beside her.

'The children told me you'd gone out,' he said.

'You called at the house?' She was going to ask him if he wanted to speak to her about something in particular, but he replied quickly:

'Yes and no. They were both in the garden. Richard was just about to go and see Colin — Lisa refused to go with him, so she's on her own. I thought I'd better fetch you. I guessed that you would have come this way.'

'I was just going back. I doubt if Lisa

would get up to any mischief if she's left on her own for a few minutes . . .'

'Probably not,' said Toby, adding rather intensely, 'but if anything happened to either of you, I should never forgive myself!'

'Aren't you being rather melodramatic?' she asked. 'In any case, isn't Mr Bagster in the garden? He seems to spend most of his time about the place.'

'No. He told me he was going to Stirbridge to get a bolt for one of the doors. He's not back yet.'

They walked a little way in silence before he asked her, far too casually, 'Who were you talking to just now?'

'Why? Does it matter?'

'I just wondered. He didn't look like anybody I know.'

'No? Actually, he's a visitor. I think he's staying at the pub in Petercliffe. It's all right — he's not a stranger. I used to know him, years ago.'

'A friend of yours? That's all right, then. Did he know you were living here?'

'No — it's pure coincidence. We happened to meet the other day. He's not a particularly close friend, or anything like that. We used to work together at one time.'

'An actor?'

'Not now. He tells me he's an antique dealer.'

'Another variety of rogue!' he said, with grim humour.

'There's no need to be rude,' she reproved him.

'Perhaps not.' She would almost have thought he was a little jealous.

'It's very kind of you to take so much interest in our welfare,' she said, not without irony.

'I should be far happier about you — and Lisa — if your husband were not so far away. You really need someone to take care of you, Mrs Markham.' All the time he was speaking to her, his eyes were giving her some kind of message; his concern was obviously far greater than his actual words revealed. Her heart gave a lurch:

he was so different from Peter! If only she had met him in different circumstances . . . She pulled herself together.

'Will you come back and have some tea with us, Mr Anderson? I expect Lisa will be very pleased to see you.'

'Thank you — I'd like to.'

There was no sign of Lisa when they went into the house. After a moment, Valerie called, 'I'm back! Where are you? Mr Anderson's here.'

'Coming!' Lisa called from upstairs. They heard a door slam and then Lisa came down, looking cross and rather flustered.

'What's the matter?' asked Valerie. 'Has Richard done something to upset you?'

'He's a beast!' exclaimed Lisa. 'One of these days, I'll kill him!'

'Whatever has he done?' asked Toby. As Lisa did not answer, Valerie spoke for her. 'I expect it's because he prefers Colin's company to hers. Not to mention the ferrets.'

'Confound the ferrets,' said Lisa in

such a deep, grownup voice that Toby and Valerie started to laugh.

'You can talk to Mr Anderson while I put the kettle on,' suggested Valerie.

'Why do you always call him 'Mr Anderson'?' asked Lisa. 'He lets me call him Toby.'

'Because he always calls me 'Ms Markam'. It's more polite.'

'Just as it's more polite for you to say 'Mummy' instead of calling your mother by her Christian name,' added Toby.

'I don't!' protested Lisa.

'Oh yes, you do! I've heard you!'

'Sorry,' said Lisa, 'I forgot.'

'It really doesn't matter.' Valerie smiled. 'Why don't we all agree to be thoroughly modern? I like Lisa to call me 'Valerie' — it makes me feel younger. So why don't you call me 'Valerie' too? And then I can call you 'Toby' — if you don't object.'

'Younger!' he snorted. 'You've no need to worry about that. You don't look much more than a schoolgirl.'

'She's quite old really,' said Lisa. 'She'll be thirty tomorrow. I wanted her to have a birthday party, but she says grown-up people don't go in for that sort of thing. I think she's ashamed of being so old.'

'Toby shall have tea with us today instead,' said Valerie hastily. 'In any case, Mr Wagstaff is coming to see me tomorrow afternoon. On business, so it wouldn't be convenient to have a party. . .'

'What on earth does he want?' Lisa did not sound too pleased.

'Never you mind, young lady,' said Valerie. 'It's no concern of yours. And I've already told you that when your daddy comes home, we will have a proper party.'

'A big one? And will Toby come? And Peter?'

'Of course we shall invite Toby. But I expect Peter will have gone back to London by that time.' Valerie certainly hoped so: he was becoming rather a nuisance.

Richard did not return to West Lodge until after they had finished their tea and Toby had gone. When she saw him, Lisa went red and she looked very angry again. Her brother either did not notice or chose to ignore her bad temper. To Valerie's relief, the explosion she expected never came. Whatever Richard had done to annoy her, Lisa had decided that discretion was the better part of valour.

When Bagster arrived with the new bolt, he insisted on fitting it at once, in spite of Valerie's protests.

'Can't it wait until Monday? We've done without it for so long that two more days shouldn't make any difference.'

'No, Mrs Markham. I've brought it, so I might as well do it straight away. I'm sure that, if Mr Wagstaff had realized there wasn't a bolt on that door, he would have insisted some time ago. It won't take me long, and I shan't get in your way.'

Valerie capitulated, thinking that she

should be thankful that Mr Wagstaff hadn't arranged for all the doors to be bolted on the outside as well, to prevent her from escaping! Although Toby had obviously enjoyed her company at tea-time, she suspected that the main reason for accepting her invitation was that he had been told to keep an eye on her until Bagster came back from Stirbridge.

That evening, Valerie and the children watched television. She was glad when they agreed to have an early night. Lisa hardly spoke to Richard the whole evening, although he seemed unaware that he had done anything to upset her.

When Valerie had been round the house, checking the locks and bolts, she decided to go to bed early herself. As soon as she was in her room, however, she immediately began to feel restless.

She tried not to think of such things when she was with the children but, to be honest with herself, she had started to worry about Mrs Spenser's apparent disappearance. She had never doubted that Mr Wagstaff was seriously concerned about the old lady's welfare and the marchesa's decision to come to Greenleafe must mean that she shared his anxiety.

Valerie's own grandmother had, at the age of seventy-five, suddenly decided that she wanted to visit Petra and had gone on an expedition to visit the 'rose red city, half as old as time', without bothering to mention it to any of her family. Grandma Markham was an exceptional woman, who had spent many years travelling round the world with her husband, who was, like his son and his grandson, a dedicated scientist. She thought nothing of making trips to remote places, and it had seemed reasonable to assume that Mrs Spenser was the same sort of person. Now she was not so sure: from what Mr Wagstaff and Toby had told her and since she had learnt of Mrs Spenser's heart condition, Valerie admitted that she was unlikely to have changed her plans without telling any of her friends.

Valerie lay awake for some time, worrying. The house that night was exceptionally quiet — so quiet that something about the very silence filled her with foreboding.

8

'Happy birthday, Val!' said Lisa with a smile. She had brought early morning tea. Valerie sat up in bed, noticing that the tea was in one of the best china cups — she was thankful that it had arrived safely and without any being spilt on the fine linen traycloth. Beside the saucer, Lisa had placed a single red rosebud in a crystal vase and an envelope, which Valerie opened at once. It was a birthday card from the children.

'We'll give you your presents when you come downstairs.'

'I suppose what you mean is that you want me to hurry up and get dressed, because you both want your breakfast!' Valerie laughed.

'Not really — but Richard's started getting the breakfast. It's supposed to be a surprise — but it would be a pity if it went cold before you arrived.'

'You're spoiling me! By the way, have you and Richard made up your quarrel?'

'Sort of. I still think he's a beast.'

'Never mind — lots of boys are, from time to time. And girls can be just as beastly when they set their minds to it.'

'I suppose so. Are you cross with me?'

'Of course not! Why should I be? Have you got a guilty conscience about something then, Lisa?'

'N-no. Oh, please come downstairs soon, Val! I want you to see your present.'

The breakfast was very good, although Richard had boiled the eggs a little longer than Valerie would have liked. The toast was not burnt and the coffee was excellent.

She opened Richard's parcel first. As she expected, it contained a book. A cookery book — he certainly had a practical nature. She wondered if he thought her cooking needed improvement and, when she had thanked him, she asked as much.

'Goodness, no! You mustn't think that — you're a much better cook than Mums. I've bought her a cookery book, too — but she'll have to wait until she gets back from Brazil. I can't very well send it to her.'

'I haven't bought her present yet,' confessed Lisa. 'Aren't you going to open yours, Val? I do hope you like it.'

Carefully Valerie untied the ribbon round the tiny parcel and folded the scrap of wrapping paper to reveal a cardboard box, lined with pale green tissue. Inside was a fine gold chain with a pendant: she gasped when she saw it. The green stone could easily have passed for an emerald, except that an unflawed gem of that size would have cost a fortune. Looking at it closely, Valerie could almost believe that it was genuine. The small crystals which adorned the ornate gold setting looked equally convincing, sparkling with the cold fire of real diamonds.

'Wherever did you get this, Lisa? It's gorgeous!'

'I bought the chain in Stirbridge yesterday. I'm afraid it's only gold-plated . . .'

'What about the pendant?'

'She found it in the wood!' sneered Richard. 'It was lying under a tree. Of course, it isn't real.'

'It could be,' said Lisa angrily. 'You don't know.'

'Don't be stupid. Nobody wears an emerald that size to go for a country walk. It's obviously a fake.'

'Why do you always spoil things?' asked Lisa. 'Do you think it's a fake, Val?'

'Honestly, dear, it must be. But never mind, Lisa — that doesn't matter at all. It's beautiful and I shall enjoy wearing it.'

'There!' said Lisa to her brother, 'I told you she'd like it. But wouldn't it be wonderful if it did turn out to be real, after all . . .'

'That would create problems, Lisa. Apart from being very valuable, and costing a great deal of money to insure, whoever lost it would certainly want it back. They'd give a description of it to the police and then, if anybody saw me wearing it, they'd think I'd stolen it. At the very least, I'd have to give it back, and it's so pretty I want to keep it. Where exactly did you find it, Lisa?'

'In the long grass by the side of the road, when I was looking for Peter's lighter.'

'What did he think about it?' Valerie reckoned that, if he had seen it, it was a wonder he hadn't claimed it and taken it away to sell in his shop.

'I didn't tell him about it. I only showed it to Richard — and he said it was broken and I'd better throw it away. There was nothing to hang it on, you see. But when I bought the chain, the man in the shop sold me two little gold rings and I used those to fix it.'

'You mean that I did,' said Richard. 'You had to ask me to help.'

'You're better than I am with pliers and things,' admitted Lisa. 'Aren't you going to wear it, Val?'

'I shall this afternoon. I don't want it to get lost again while I'm rushing round the house.'

'You do really like it?'

'Of course I do! It's a lovely present.'

Later that morning, while she was in the kitchen icing the cake for the children's tea — the only concession she was making to Lisa's idea that her birthday was a cause for celebration — there was a tap on the door.

'Come in! It isn't locked.'

Toby came in and handed her a parcel, muttering, 'For you!'

She put down the icing bag, wiped her hands on her apron and undid the wrapping. It was another book: *Dales Bestiary — the fauna of the Yorkshire Dales*, by T. F. Anderson. It was a moment before it dawned on her that Toby was the author.

'Yours?'

'Yes, I wrote it some years ago. It

started as a thesis — I'd been doing some post-graduate work at Cambridge. Then someone suggested that it might be of general interest, so I rewrote it. As you and your family know the Dales so well . . . '

'Thank you. I'm sure I shall enjoy reading it.' She laid it on the dresser, out of harm's way. 'Now, if you don't mind waiting a couple of minutes while I finish icing this cake, perhaps you'd like a glass of sherry. Unless you're in a hurry to go off anywhere?'

'No. Thank you, I'd love a glass of sherry! Where are the children?'

'They've both cycled down to Petercliffe to buy some chocolate biscuits. They find my birthday far more exciting than I do, I'm afraid. Being thirty fills me with horror.'

'Why ever should it, Valerie? After all, I'm nearly ten years older than that and I certainly don't feel any older than I did when I was at school.'

'It's different for a man.'

'Why ever should it be? Of course, no

doubt being married changes the way one feels.'

'You're not married? Have you been?'

'No. Until recently, I've never met anyone I wanted to share my life with.'

'Until recently?'

'Yes — unfortunately, in the end, I did meet somebody.'

'Unfortunately?'

'Yes — it happened too late.'

'Doesn't she feel the same way about you?'

'No. I wouldn't expect her to — she's married to somebody else. Even if she did care about me, any relationship between us would be out of the question. It's a question of loyalty, you see.'

'Is her husband a friend of yours?'

'No — I've never met him. But she must be completely loyal to him, of course, so I could never tell her how I felt about her. Marriage is a permanent relationship, you see — a contract for life.'

'Not always. People have been known

to make mistakes.'

'Then that's their misfortune. If I had ever married, it would have been for keeps. And this woman I met — suppose I had told her how I felt about her and had persuaded her to leave her husband and come away with me, how could I ever be certain that she wouldn't change her mind again and go off with someone else altogether? Besides, I don't think I could live with the thought that I'd stolen another man's wife.'

'Stolen her? What an old-fashioned idea! It sounds as if you think that a wife is simply her husband's property.'

'No, I don't. No more than I think that he is *her* property! Perhaps I am old-fashioned: I do realize that many people nowadays look at these things quite differently. You, for instance. You're an actress. I do realize that, in your scheme of things, relationships are far more casual than they are in mine.'

'Not necessarily,' Valerie spoke cautiously. What was he trying to tell her?

Was she reading too much into the expression in those dark eyes? She felt the blood rising to her face as she said, 'That's how I've always felt, too. When I was very young, I made up my mind that I would only get married when I knew I'd met someone with whom I was prepared to spend the rest of my life.'

'You didn't have to look far,' said Toby. 'You found your cousin! I envy you both.'

A few minutes after Richard and Lisa had returned with the biscuits, Toby made his excuses and left, leaving Valerie feeling dismayed and confused. Had he been trying to tell her that *she* was the woman he had been looking for all his life? Did he realize that she was in love with him? And was he warning her off?

'What's this?' Lisa picked up the *Dales Bestiary* and looked at it curiously.

'Toby gave it to me: he wrote it himself.'

Lisa was looking inside it. 'He's put something in it, too.'

'Let me see!' Valerie's hand shook slightly as she took the book and looked at the message on the title page. 'For Valerie Markham, with best wishes from Toby'. That was all — well, she could hardly expect him to write, 'With all my love', could she? So far as Toby was concerned, even if she had not imagined his feelings about her, she was taboo — Alex's wife and Lisa's mother.

And when the children's real parents arrived from Brazil? Then Toby would realize that she had deceived him — lied to him from the very beginning. The deception would assuredly destroy any tender feelings he might have towards her. He had such a highly developed sense of honour — she could never live up to it! It was no good trying to tell herself that the man was simply a prig — she didn't really believe it and, in any case, she really was in love with him.

Not knowing exactly when Mr

Wagstaff and the marchesa would arrive, they had lunch early and then Valerie went up to her room to change. To please Lisa, she would wear something more dressy than usual: the child was determined to make a big occasion out of her birthday. The wardrobe in her room was nearly full of Vanessa's clothes. She had, of course, brought them with her; most of her own had been left in her flat. The only suitable dress she had brought with her was a simple sheath of raw silk, with a matching jacket. Usually she wore her pearls with it — the single string which her mother had given her when she was eighteen — but today she would wear the pendant Lisa had given her.

The green pendant looked stunning against the pale, shimmering silk. Valerie collected costume jewellery, choosing each piece with her usual fastidiousness, but she had never had anything of this quality. For a fake, it was superb. Too showy for a business meeting, of course! Ruefully, she slipped it underneath her dress. When the visitors left, she would give Lisa the pleasure of seeing her wear it. Before she left her room, she dabbed a few drops of her favourite scent on her pulse points . . .

Lisa was looking bored and lost when Valerie went downstairs. Richard had gone off to see Colin, leaving his sister at a loose end. Valerie thought of telling her to go and play in the garden but she felt too sorry for the little girl. Why should she be pushed out of the way? So she took her into the kitchen to help her prepare a tea tray. A buzzer sounded and, looking up, Valerie saw a small telltale bobbing up and down in the box on the wall which held the old-fashioned electric bell system. It was in the window marked 'Front Door', so the visitors must have arrived. Neither Valerie nor Lisa had seen the gadget working before and they both found it very amusing.

Mr Wagstaff was waiting on the step with a tall, willowy woman whose cornflower blue linen suit matched her eyes. She had silver-blonde hair and, Valerie thought, a thin, mean-looking mouth. However, she smiled at Valerie and took the arm of the third member of the party.

'I hope you don't mind, Mrs Markham,' said the solicitor, indicating Toby. 'Mr Anderson is a close friend of Mrs Spenser's, so we thought it was a good idea for him to come too.'

The more the merrier, thought Valerie, wondering why Toby had not mentioned in the morning that he was to be one of the party. Valerie was introduced to the marchesa and then they all joined Lisa in the small sitting-room.

'Your daughter, Mrs Markham?' The marchesa swooped on the child and stared at her. 'She's exactly like you! And what's your name, little girl? My Antonia is about your age — what a pity I didn't bring her with me.'

'Does she speak Italian?' asked Lisa. 'Or English?'

'Both!' said the marchesa.

'Go and see if the kettle's boiling yet,' suggested Valerie, 'and, when it does, I'm sure the marchesa and Mr Wagstaff would like some tea. And Toby, of course. Get out another cup.'

'What a lovely idea!' smiled the other woman. She turned to Toby. 'Why didn't you tell me about the little girl? She's sweet. Is she your only child, Mrs Markham?'

'Alex was married before,' replied Valerie truthfully, 'so Lisa has a half brother . . . he's gone to see his friend. Lisa does spend a lot of time with me; I hope she won't be in the way.'

'Of course not.' The marchesa lowered her voice. 'I was dreadfully sorry to hear about poor old Mrs Gregory. It was quite a shock — I'd known her ever since we — since I was a child. She lived in, of course, before she married Gregory. She must have worked for my mother for over forty years. Mama is going to be dreadfully upset when she hears what happened to her. I believe it was you who found her?'

'No — it was the boy, Richard,' said Toby.

'Was he very upset, Mrs Markham?'

'No, I don't think so. He's quite tough, Mar . . .'

'Please, do call me Angela! And you're Vanessa, aren't you?'

'No, my name's Valerie. Vanessa is my sister.'

'Oh? Then Mama must have got you muddled up. No doubt you told her you have a sister . . .'

'When we've had our cup of tea,' said Mr Wagstaff, 'I expect you will want to have a look in your mother's room. Perhaps Mrs Markham will tell us where to find the key.'

'Now we're here, there's no actual hurry, is there?' asked the marchesa doubtfully. Valerie glanced at her face. Under the mask of bright sociability was something very different. She realized that Angela was frightened.

Lisa came in with the tray. This time, she had not used the best china, but she arranged the chocolate biscuits prettily on a silver dish. Angela exclaimed with delight — Antonia, she said, would never have done anything so useful. She was neither so grown-up nor so helpful as Lisa. The child looked embarrassed for a moment. Then she smiled. 'It looks as if we're having a birthday party after all,' she said happily.

'Is it your birthday, then?' asked the marchesa. 'How old are you, dear?'

'No — it's not my birthday. It's Val's. She's thirty.'

The marchesa gave a tinkling laugh, which was followed by a moment's embarrassed silence. Then Lisa said, 'Why aren't you wearing your prezzie? I thought you were going to put it on after lunch.'

'I am wearing it — but it's a bit early in the day to display the crown jewels. It's under my frock.'

'Don't be silly,' snorted Lisa, 'you ought to show it off — it will go nicely with that dress.' She reached out and fished out the pendant from beneath

Valerie's bodice. 'There!' she said. 'Doesn't that look lovely?'

The marchesa stared at Valerie and gave a little shriek. The tea cup fell out of her hand on to the floor.

'What on earth's the matter?' asked Toby.

'Go and get a cloth to mop up that tea, Lisa,' said Valerie, 'before it stains the carpet.' Lisa hurried from the room.

The marchesa had gone white. She strode across to Valerie and took hold of the pendant, asking in a terrible voice, 'Where did you get this?'

'It was a birthday present. Lisa gave it to me.'

'I don't believe you,' said the marchesa.

'Angela!' interrupted Toby. 'Whatever's the matter?'

'It's just a piece of costume jewellery,' said Valerie.

'Oh, no it isn't — as I should know. You'd better tell me where it really came from, Mrs Markham. And I want the truth.'

'I've told you the truth. Of course, if you must know, Lisa didn't buy it. She found it in the forest.'

'A likely story,' sneered the marchesa. 'Wag! Call the police!'

'Just a moment, my dear,' said the solicitor. 'Before I do anything drastic, hadn't you better explain what's the matter?'

'Very well. This woman is wearing something which belongs to me.'

'Don't be ridiculous,' said Valerie. 'How can it? In any case, it's only costume jewellery. It's just a fake emerald pendant that Lisa found lying where some visitor had dropped it. It can't possibly be yours — you were in Italy at the time.'

'Nevertheless, it's mine. And it isn't a fake — I should have thought that any fool could see that! It's the drop from one of my mother's ear-rings. She said she was going to give me her emeralds, as she wasn't likely to wear them again. She was going to bring them to Italy with her. If she'd left them to me in her will, I should have had to pay a fortune in death duties.'

'If this is true,' said Valerie, 'can you prove it?'

'More easily than you think,' replied the marchesa, walking over to a glass-fronted bookcase which stood on a bureau in the corner of the room. She opened the door, but could not quite reach the top shelf.

'Let me,' said Toby. 'What do you want?'

'That book with the red leather binding,' said the marchesa.

It was a photograph album. She took it, turning the pages until she came to a full-page studio portrait, which she showed to Valerie. It was of a middle-aged woman, handsome rather than beautiful, with a distinctly aristocratic bearing. She had pale blonde hair and blue eyes which were almost colourless. Of course, Valerie had never met the woman but, immediately she saw the photograph, she had the feeling that it was the portrait of someone she knew.

However, far more to the point was the jewellery she was wearing — a magnificent collar of emeralds and diamonds, with a matching tiara and bracelets. And a pair of superb earrings. Valerie took off the pendant she was wearing to compare it with the photograph. There was no doubt that the marchesa was telling the truth — what Lisa had found was one of those beautiful emerald drops.

'I suppose you intended to sell the rest of the set?' asked the marchesa. 'You'd better give this to me. Then you can tell us where you've put the rest of the things — and how you managed to get hold of them.'

'Hold on!' said Mr Wagstaff. 'You really mustn't jump to conclusions, Angela my dear. I expect there's some perfectly innocent explanation . . .'

'Don't be such an old fool!' snapped the marchesa. 'You're almost as bad as my mother. She has an equally idiotic faith in human nature.'

Lisa came in from the kitchen with a bowl of warm water and a cloth. Seeing the pendant in the marchesa's hand, she said innocently, 'Isn't it heavenly? I knew Val would like it. She loves pretty things.'

'You knew? So where did you get it?'

'In the wood. I didn't think it would matter that I hadn't bought it — I did buy the chain. Why?'

'Do you know what happens to children who don't tell the truth?'

'I am telling the truth,' said Lisa stoutly.

'I don't think you are, my dear.'

Puzzled, Lisa looked from the marchesa to Valerie and back again. Then she blurted out, 'It *is* the truth: I can show you exactly where I found it. Why don't you believe me? Anyway, it isn't a real emerald — Richard said so.'

'Leave her alone!' Valerie turned on the marchesa. 'You're frightening her.'

'I'll do a lot more than that before I've finished!' The other woman was livid with anger. 'My mother would never leave part of her ear-ring lying under a tree, now would she? If you really did find it, child, you'd better tell me where. Was it in my mother's room? And what have you done with the rest of the emeralds?'

'I found it in the wood,' repeated Lisa, 'and there weren't any other things.'

'The best thing,' said Mr Wagstaff gently, 'is to do what we came here for. We'll go upstairs to Mrs Spenser's room and find out if she's left a note. Let me take charge of this for the time being.' He took the pendant, wrapped it carefully in his handkerchief and put it in his top pocket.

'Now, Mrs Markham, if you will be kind enough to show us where the key is . . . '

Lisa gave a little cry and dashed out of the room. Valerie was going to follow her, but the marchesa grabbed her by the wrist.

'No, you don't!' she said. 'You're coming with us.' Valerie heard the front door slam shut but there was obviously nothing she could do, so she led the others into the pantry.

'There's a step ladder . . . ' she begun, but Toby assured her that he could reach the top shelf when she pointed out the pewter cup to him. He handed it down to Mr Wagstaff.

'Are you certain that this is where Mrs Gregory put the key?' asked the solicitor. He showed Valerie the cup. It was empty.

9

'There!' said the marchesa angrily.

Valerie was horrified. 'I don't understand. That's where it was.'

'I think your little girl knows something about it,' said the other woman. 'We'd better go and find out what else she's taken.'

'Lisa is not a thief.'

'No? I wouldn't trust her . . . and I don't trust you either, Mrs Markham.'

The solicitor cleared his throat. 'Angela!' he warned her. 'You should be careful what you say. Mrs Markham is your mother's tenant: she has excellent references, which I checked myself. You really mustn't jump to conclusions and start accusing her . . . '

'References can be faked!' said the marchesa.

Far more likely, Valerie was thinking, that Richard had taken that key. He would no more have stolen anything than his sister but he had just as much curiosity and was far less timid. It would not surprise her if Richard had decided to look inside the locked room. He had probably forgotten to replace the key.

'You had better come upstairs with us,' said the marchesa. 'I should prefer you to be with us when we open the door, Mrs Markham, especially as we are going to have to force the lock.'

'Shall I ask Bagster for some tools?' asked Toby. 'The doors in this house are very solid.'

'Let's go and look first,' said Mr Wagstaff, calm as ever. 'It's quite possible that drastic action might not be necessary.' They all trooped upstairs and, when they had reached the door of Mrs Spenser's room, he tried the handle. The door swung open easily.

This was not at all what Valerie had expected but, after a moment's thought, she remembered what had happened the previous afternoon. When she and

Toby came into the house, Lisa had been upstairs. In answer to her call, the child had run downstairs looking very bothered. Valerie also remembered hearing a door slam.

Mr Wagstaff went into the room, followed closely by the marchesa and Toby, while Valerie remained outside. She heard the marchesa give a kind of snarl before rushing out again, her eyes blazing.

'Now you will have some explaining to do, Mrs Markham.' She seized Valerie's arm and dragged her through the door.

A four-poster bed, even larger than the one in Valerie's room, with its curtains drawn shut, was the only thing in the room which did not look as if a tornado had struck it. Chairs had been overturned, drawers pulled out and their contents strewn over the floor and all the cupboard doors hung wide open. Clothes were scattered everywhere, but of the 'little knick-knacks' Mrs Gregory had spoken about, there was no sign.

'Burglars,' said Toby. 'After all the trouble we went to!'

'What are you talking about?' asked the marchesa.

'Your mother kept telling us to make sure that the house was never left unoccupied, even for a single night. I thought she was being over-cautious, but she's an old lady and it seemed best to do what she wanted. The day she left, Bagster stayed until eight in the evening and then I took over for the rest of the night.'

'Almost as if she expected an intruder,' said Mr Wagstaff. 'Were you and Bagster actually in the house that night?'

'No. But we would certainly have seen if anyone came in or out. Nobody came anywhere near the place until Mrs Gregory arrived the next morning and she stayed until Mrs Markham and the children got here.'

'I don't think it was a burglar,' the marchesa's voice was icy and she glared at Valerie. 'That child was playing tricks. I expect she found that emerald and thought it would save her having to buy anything for you! Then she messed the place up — out of wickedness!'

'Lisa isn't like that at all,' protested Valerie.

'Then why wasn't the rest of the house ransacked? Burglars would hardly have concentrated on just one room.'

'Mrs Gregory mentioned that your mother had left a few little things in here that she didn't want to risk getting broken — china ornaments, I suppose — that sort of thing. I can't see any, can you? There seems to be nothing here except clothes.'

'Could anyone else have been playing a trick?' asked Toby. 'Leaving the room in a mess to make it look as if it had been burgled? I doubt if Mrs Spenser's treasures are very far away. Perhaps they're hidden in the bed!' And he strode across and drew aside one of the heavy curtains. Then he gasped, 'Oh, good heavens!'

'What is it?' Mr Wagstaff and the marchesa went closer to look. Then she screamed loudly.

Valerie saw a slight figure lying on the bed, under the counterpane, with its head turned towards them. There was no mistaking the blue-rinsed hair spread on the pillow. But the face! Valerie felt sick.

The empty eye sockets and grinning teeth of a skull faced them, its features veiled with some hideous grey membrane which mocked the living flesh which had once filled out that hideous face. Then, suddenly, she realized exactly what it was that she was looking at. She could not help starting to laugh.

'Alas, poor Yorick!' she quoted, half hysterically. Of course, someone had taken the papier-mâché skull from the box containing the properties for *Hamlet* and had stretched a nylon stocking over it. The elegant, blue-tinted wig completed the bizarre effect.

'Who on earth would do a thing like that?' asked Mr Wagstaff, when she had explained. 'And where did that wig come from?'

The marchesa had regained her composure. 'That's one of Mother's,' she said. 'She's been more or less bald for years! I thought everyone knew that!' She turned to Valerie suspiciously, 'And how do you happen to know about that skull, Mrs Markham?'

'The boxes upstairs. When the children and I saw them, I had a look inside some of them.'

'So that's how you knew? And of course your children knew where to find it?'

'No,' said Valerie. 'When I looked in the box, the skull was missing.'

'Do you expect me to believe that? Wag — you'd better call the police. Even if it's only a stupid child who's taken my emeralds . . . '

'Your mother's emeralds, Angela,' he corrected her gently. 'She hasn't actually given them to you yet, has she, Angela?'

'As good as!' stormed the marchesa.

'They're no longer any use to her. But that little monster has obviously hidden them somewhere . . . '

'Then we should ask her where they are,' said Valerie. 'Lisa is not a thief.'

'Then perhaps you are, Mrs Markham. And where is my mother?'

'I understood she wired you to say she was going to stay in Paris for a few days.'

'Anybody could have sent that telegram.'

'Well, I certainly didn't. I don't know your address. I hadn't even heard of your existence until Mr Wagstaff mentioned you.'

'Indeed? I would have thought Mother would have told you all about me when you came to talk about the lease? Surely, she wouldn't have missed that opportunity!'

'Angela, please!' exclaimed Mr Wagstaff.

Of course, Valerie had no idea what Mrs Spenser had told Vanessa when they met, so there was nothing she could say.

'There you are!' said the marchesa triumphantly. 'When your little darling comes back, we'll get the truth out of her, one way or another.'

'I think she went out of the house,' said Toby. 'You'd better go and find her, Valerie. Would you like me to come with you?'

'Quick thinking, Toby! You'd better go with her, in case she decides to disappear.'

'How dare you!' said Valerie. 'This obscene joke has nothing to do with Lisa, or with me.'

'Please be reasonable, Angela,' said Toby. 'There's no need to treat Mrs Markham as if she were a criminal.'

'Haven't you any idea what those emeralds are worth?'

'There's no need for you to come with me, Toby,' said Valerie. 'I don't suppose she's gone very far.'

Mr Bagster was in the kitchen garden, sitting at the door of the potting shed, smoking his pipe. He had not seen Lisa in the garden and had not noticed if she went out through the gate. Valerie was not surprised; she had thought from the beginning that the child had probably gone towards the wood, so she walked along the road in that direction. She was fairly certain now that Lisa must have been in Mrs Spencer's room the previous day, though she did not think she would have touched anything. Certainly, she would never have set up that horrible dummy in the bed.

As she passed the green, Richard came out of one of the cottages and she called to him.

'Where are you going?' he asked.

'I'm trying to find Lisa. She ran out of the house. Richard — have you been playing practical jokes on her?'

'No. Why?' Was that puzzled look on his face merely a cover-up for a guilty conscience?

'Are you sure, Richard? She seems to have had quite a fright . . .'

'Do you want me to help you find her?'

'No — you'd better go back to the house. Mr Wagstaff's there with Mrs Spenser's daughter. I expect they'll ask you some questions.'

'Here! What's all this about? And what am I supposed to tell them?'

'I think,' said Valerie calmly, 'that the best thing would be to tell them the truth. About everything! And please say I'm still looking for Lisa and I want everything cleared up just as much as they do.'

'Right! But what *is* the matter, Val?'

'I can't stop now — you'll find out soon enough. I must find Lisa before she falls into one of those soak-holes.'

'She won't,' Richard tried to reassure her. 'She's far less of a baby than she pretends to be.'

As soon as Valerie entered the wood, she had to walk more slowly. There was nothing to show which way Lisa might have gone; she looked in vain for a glimpse of her pink frock between the trees. Every now and again she shouted but, apart from a faint echo, there was no reply.

This was a nightmare, reminding Valerie of her dreams that Vanessa was in danger. Now it seemed that it was not Vanessa but she herself who was threatened: she had a feeling of dread which had nothing to do with the missing emeralds or with practical jokes. Thinking about it, she realized that it would have been impossible for Richard to set up the dummy in order to scare his sister. The skull was already missing from the box in the attic when he first went up there and he could have no idea how to get hold of a blue-tinted wig. She felt that she owed him an apology — but who *had* done it?

There was no sign of Lisa near the deer tower, nor when she approached the ramshackle hut. Could that be where she was hiding? Doubtful; but she had better make sure. She walked round it until she reached the path through the brambles. They had grown back since she had last seen them and the nettles were taller than she remembered. A broken stem near the edge of the path showed that someone had been that way recently, so she hoped that her search was nearly over. With a sigh of relief, she entered the hut.

'Surprise, surprise!' Peter rose from the tea chest on which he was sitting. 'To what do I owe the pleasure of this visit?'

'Have you seen Lisa?'

'I'm sorry, no.' He shook his head. 'I thought you didn't allow her out by herself nowadays.'

'I don't. But she ran out of the house and I thought she might have come this way.'

'Has she been getting into trouble?'

'I'm sure it's only a misunderstanding.'

'Tell me about it. Then I'll help you look for her.'

Valerie blurted out what had happened. When she explained about the emerald pendant, he stopped her.

'She found it in the wood?'

'Yes. Of course, she had no idea it was genuine. She bought a little gold chain and gave it to me for a present.'

'Have you got it? I should like to see it.'

'I'm afraid you can't . . .'

As he stared at her, and she looked back at him, she had a sudden revelation. She made herself smile, hoping that he had not noticed the start of recognition she gave when she looked into those pale blue eyes. Of course! That was why the photograph of Mrs Spenser had seemed so familiar. The eyes, the mouth, the beautifully modelled features were identical. This man, whom she knew as 'Peter' must be Simon Spenser, her landlady's son.

'Give it to me!' His voice, half wheedling, half threatening, had a sinister quality she had not noticed before.

'I haven't got it,' she faltered.

He sighed. 'Then you will have to get

it, Valerie. You see — it belongs to me.'

'How can it? I don't understand.'

'I think you do. Don't pretend, Valerie — I can see it in your eyes. You know who I am, don't you? So you'd better hand it over — it's an essential part of my little collection. Mama's emeralds won't make nearly as much as they should if one of the ear-rings is missing. So hand it over.'

'I haven't got it.' Rashly, she added, 'Your sister took it. She said it belonged to her.'

'My sister? The high and mighty Angela? Where has she sprung from?'

'She's up at the house. When she showed me a photograph of your mother, it reminded me of someone. Now that I remember all those boxes of theatrical props in the attic, I think I know . . . '

'You never were just a pretty face, were you, Valerie?' he sneered. 'Actually, I think you're too clever by half. Too clever for your own good, in any case.' Somehow, he had managed to get between her and the door. She was frightened, although she did her utmost not to show it.

'I've no idea what you're doing here, Peter — or should I call you Simon? — but surely it isn't necessary for you to skulk about in the woods? You have just as much right to be here as your sister.'

'Other people don't think so. In fact, I'm *persona non grata* at West Lodge. My ma took exception to the last show I put on at the village hall. Aladdin, it was.'

'That sounds harmless enough. Did you play Aladdin?' asked Valerie lightly. 'Or were you Abanazar — the wicked uncle?'

'Neither, my pet,' he gave a kind of giggle. 'I played Widow Twankey — in one of my mother's wigs.'

'And she objected?' Valerie was becoming increasingly uneasy. He had developed a high colour and those pale eyes were glittering feverishly.

'Didn't you ever meet my mother?

Frightfully top drawer, she was. Posh. Aristocratic, you might think. You'd imagine that she was the daughter of a duke, at the very least. She was enchanted when my sister hooked that ridiculous Italian nobleman. I wasn't good enough for her — I had vulgar friends and was always letting the side down. How much do you know about Widow Twankey, Valerie?'

'Isn't she a washerwoman?'

'That's right! Of course, when we did the panto, she was supposed to be in charge of a launderette — more up to date. So, the night when my mother condescended to see the show at the village hall, I borrowed her best wig. And her best county accent, too. And at that performance, I ad libbed about the illustrious Twankey ancestors. The audience loved it — they laughed so much it stopped the show. Of course, Ma walked out. She couldn't see the joke.'

'Why?'

'Because my grandad wasn't actually a duke, you see. Not even a marquis.

He was a real Twankey — he took in washing. When he died, he owned the biggest chain of launderettes in the Midlands — and everyone remembered him when he hadn't two ha'pennies to rub together. He bought those emeralds for her — she liked to show them off, but she kept very quiet about where the money came from. Of course, everyone knew, and when Widow Twankey started to talk about washing dirty linen in public . . . She was a real snob.'

'So are you!' said Valerie. 'But how could you be so cruel?'

'Cruel? It was hardly my fault that she couldn't take a joke. Anyway, after that she threw me out. That was when I decided to become a professional actor.' His expression changed. 'So now, I expect you'll go and tell my sister and old Wagglestick that I'm here?'

'Not if you don't want me to,' said Valerie, too quickly, adding, 'but why aren't they supposed to know? Your mother's not here.'

'Poor Mummy!' He sounded almost like a little boy.

'Why did you come back?' asked Valerie.

'To get the emeralds. I was afraid she might give them to Angela — she used to say she would. But they ought to come to me — I'm the eldest and Angela's rolling in money already. Those emeralds are worth a fortune; enough to buy everything I want. But why should I tell you? You know too much already.'

He took a step towards her, as if to take her in his arms.

'Come here!' he said in a low voice. Valerie did not move. Although she was now very frightened, she managed not to show it. Now in control of herself, she realized what a fool she had been to show him that she knew who he was and then to admit it.

'Don't be afraid.' His voice, full of menace, was yet scarcely more than a whisper.

'Why should I be?'

He chuckled. 'That old fool Mrs Gregory wasn't afraid of me, either. She was so pleased to see me that she jumped off her bicycle and practically fell into my arms, the silly old cow.'

Valerie should have guessed that Mrs Gregory would never have stopped to talk to a stranger. The police must have realized this; otherwise they would not have suspected Jim, who was known to be popular in the neighbourhood. The last thing Mrs Gregory would have expected was to be attacked — pushed down those steps and her head battered in with a stone.

'Come here!' said Simon Spenser again, his voice as chilling as the look in those pale eyes. He took another step towards her and reached for her throat. Then she screamed and tried to beat him off, realizing with mounting horror how much stronger he was than she had ever imagined.

'Well, well, well,' said a deep voice from the doorway. 'Thieves falling out?'

Spenser swivelled round to face Toby.

He gave a crazy little giggle, asking, 'Who the hell are you? Can't you see you're interrupting a private conversation?'

'I suppose you could call it that,' said Toby scornfully.

'What else? Valerie and I are old friends.'

'Oh? Of course, I know who you are — you are exactly like your mother. Why don't you come along to West Lodge and say hello to Angela? She'll probably be pleased to see you.'

Spenser pushed Valerie aside and leapt towards the door, catapulting into Toby and knocking him over. Then he bounded out of the hut and disappeared among the trees. Valerie knelt beside Toby.

'Are you all right?' she asked anxiously. Toby ignored the question and rose to his feet.

'So that's the man you say is an old friend of yours!' he said angrily. 'That accounts for a lot.'

'He isn't a friend,' snapped Valerie,

'and until I saw that photograph, I had no idea who he really was. Thank heaven you came when you did — I think he was going to kill me.'

'Very likely. And it would have served you right. You should know better than to get mixed up with a character like that. How did you meet him? Were you at the clinic, too?'

'I don't know what you mean.'

'Isn't it obvious how sick he is? I suppose you don't care. You were very clever to persuade Mrs Markham to let you look after the children. I gather from Richard that you're not who you say you are, so you needn't go on with that little farce.'

'Vanessa Markham is my sister.'

'Really? Well, I think you'd better come back to the house. Wagstaff wants to talk to you.'

'What about Simon Spenser?'

'When we tell the police that there's a dangerous lunatic at large, they'll come and root him out. The local men know Greenleafe very well and, if necessary, they'll bring dogs.'

'And Lisa? She's wandering about by herself. I should never forgive myself if anything happened to her . . .'

'What a pity you didn't think of that before. But tell me, Valerie. Did you really think Spenser would share the loot with you? You know what those emeralds are worth — obviously enough to make you betray your sister's trust — if Mrs Markham really is your sister — and put that lovely little girl in danger. And tell lie after lie!'

'Don't be so stupid!' By this time, Valerie was really angry. 'I knew nothing about those emeralds until this afternoon, any more than I knew who Peter — Simon — really is. How could I?'

'If it were not for your elastic ideas about the nature of truth, I might believe you,' said Toby. 'I wish I could! Now I'm going to take you back to West Lodge — and start looking for Lisa myself.'

* * *

Mr Wagstaff listened quietly to Valerie's account of her deception. He did not interrupt her or make any comment until she had finished, when he asked her gently, 'Why didn't Mrs Markham tell us she'd changed her mind about joining her husband in Brazil?'

Valerie sighed. 'Because she'd undertaken to stay put. She told me about the agreement she signed . . .'

'Did she show it to you?'

Valerie shook her head, 'She explained it to me.'

'Then I'm afraid she got hold of the wrong end of the stick, young lady — and so did young Richard. What your sister signed was an undertaking not to sub-let or to leave West Lodge in the charge of any employee of hers as long as my client was away. You are neither her employee nor a sub-lessee, but a member of her family. So obviously, the agreement doesn't apply to you.'

Valerie sighed. If only she had realized, there would have been no need for any prevarication or tampering with the truth.

Mr Wagstaff took the emerald pendant out of his pocket and unwrapped it. 'What about this?' he asked. 'There's no doubt that it is part of Mrs Spenser's ear-ring. If your niece really did find it in the forest, I should like to know how it got there. I imagine that Simon had something to do with it. How well do you know him?'

'Not at all well really. He was just a man I used to work with, some years ago. I knew him as Peter. I had no idea he was Mrs Spenser's son. Please believe me!'

'I think I do, my dear. I'd better explain exactly why we're all so worried about him — and his mother. Simon has always been mentally unstable. Eventually, his condition deteriorated so much that Mrs Spenser realized that he needed institutional care, so she arranged for him to live in a private clinic rather than an ordinary mental hospital. Just before she was to leave for Italy, the doctor in charge of the clinic telephoned her to say that Simon had absconded. Apparently she did not tell the doctor she was going away . . . '

'That must have been the man I spoke to, soon after we came here,' said Valerie. 'I put him on to you.'

'Quite so. And two days after Mrs Spenser heard from him, she left for Italy, as she had planned. The day before, she deposited her jewellery in the bank in Stirbridge, apart from the emeralds, which she may have intended to give to Angela. On both occasions, several people saw her leave West Lodge in a hired car. She did not tell anyone that she had changed her plans and she spoke to no one. Bagster was in the garden the morning she left but, although he half expected her to give him some last minute instructions, she left without a word.'

'Do you think Simon had already arrived here when she left?'

'No,' said Mr Wagstaff, 'I should have expected her to let me know if anything untoward had happened, but she didn't get in touch with me either.'

'Is Simon the reason she made such a fuss about security?'

'Yes indeed. He is potentially dangerous and even Mrs Spenser realized that, if he turned up here, his presence would constitute a risk. You can see why we're all so worried about her. Of course, if she had not actually been seen leaving for the airport . . .'

'Toby — Mr Anderson — thinks the police will soon find Simon,' said Valerie. 'I hope he's right! Thank you for explaining everything to me. And thank you for believing me! I'm sorry about the deception — I suppose it isn't surprising that Mr Anderson thinks the worst of me.'

'No doubt he'll get over it.'

'I realize now that I should never have agreed to take Vanessa's place.'

'You mustn't blame yourself, Miss Markham. If your sister had been here herself, I doubt if things would have turned out very differently.' Behind his half moon spectacles, his eyes looked at her benevolently — almost approvingly.

If only Toby's reaction had been like that. Even if he realized now that she could not have been Simon Spenser's accomplice, she knew that he despised her. She realized how important to him was honesty — a quality which he believed she lacked.

'Don't worry about Mr Anderson,' said Mr Wagstaff. 'As soon as he finds Lisa, I'm sure everything will be all right.'

Valerie wished she shared his confidence.

10

Greenleafe was buzzing with police vehicles. Valerie was questioned by a very sympathetic plain-clothes officer. She told him what had happened and repeated what Simon had told her about the death of Mrs Gregory and soon a full-scale search for him was under way. In the middle of it all, Toby arrived at West Lodge with a grubby and tearful Lisa. He had found her hiding in the deer tower — she had seen Simon running away from the hut and was going to greet him when something in the expression of his face warned her to keep well clear of him.

'So Wagstaff swallowed your story?' Toby, stony-faced, asked Valerie. 'And what about the police?'

'I told the truth,' said Valerie. He did not reply, but turned his back on her and strode away towards the forest office.

Mr Wagstaff was reluctant to leave Valerie and the children alone in West Lodge, although the marchesa was impatient to get back to the hotel in Stirbridge. After she had flounced out of the house in the direction of his car, the solicitor asked Valerie, 'Are you sure you'll be all right? I could ask Mr Anderson to come back and stay in the house with you tonight.'

'That's quite unnecessary,' she reassured him. 'The forest is swarming with police, so we're unlikely to come to any harm. Please don't worry about us, Mr Wagstaff.'

However, as soon as they had driven away, she felt shivery and apprehensive. She sent Lisa upstairs to get washed and changed, while she started to prepare the evening meal. She called Richard.

'Come into the kitchen — I want to talk to you.' She closed the door behind them and asked him in a low voice,

'What on earth made you persuade Lisa to go into Mrs Spenser's room?'

'I didn't! I was only teasing her; I told her she wouldn't dare!'

'Well, she did dare.'

'What was Mr Wagstaff saying about some sort of bogle in the bed? You don't suppose I put it there, do you?'

'I wondered. You know how she said she was afraid of skeletons. I thought at first you'd been playing a prank on her.' She told him about the dummy.

'But that's stupid!' Richard was indignant. 'She hasn't been scared of anything like that for ages! Dad took her to the Natural History Museum — started her off on dinosaurs and, by the time they got to a collection of human skulls, she realized they were just a lot of old bones! You know, Val, she really is a whole lot tougher than you think she is! She'd be quite capable of rigging up a dummy like that herself, if she thought it would scare anybody!'

'You didn't do it; I'm sure Lisa didn't, so who did?' mused Valerie and it was not until the three of them were eating their evening meal that the answer dawned on her.

She remembered when it was that Lisa had spoken of her fear of skeletons. The child had said that she *used* to be afraid of them and Valerie had jumped to the conclusion that she was ashamed to admit that she still was. Had the same thought occurred to Simon? Had he guessed that Lisa's curiosity might draw her into his mother's room? He could have prepared an unpleasant surprise for her to ensure that she would be too frightened to go there again or to tell anyone else what she had found there, or that the room had been ransacked.

How had he managed to get into the room himself? She knew that no one had told him where the key was hidden. And how had he been able to get into the house? Could it have been that afternoon when the children had gone to Oakham with Toby and she was sitting alone in the garden? He had come in without being seen: the house doors were open and Bagster was not about. He had probably been looking for that missing emerald . . .

'What about your birthday cake?' Lisa interrupted her thoughts. 'Aren't we going to eat it?'

'I'd forgotten all about that!' laughed Valerie. 'You'd better go and fetch it.'

'Those visitors should have stayed to tea,' said Richard.

'I'm very glad that lady didn't,' said Lisa. 'She was horrid.' A sentiment with which Valerie entirely agreed.

Later that evening, a police sergeant called to tell them that they were giving up the search in the wood, but that they intended to return the following day.

'Haven't you found him?' asked Valerie.

'No, Madam. He seems to have given us the slip. He's probably in another part of the forest. At one time, we thought the dogs were on to something. We took one of them to the hut and she started sniffing. She led us round a bit, but it turned out to be a false trail. After a while, she brought us back here. You haven't seen anyone?'

Valerie shook her head 'I should think this is the last place he'd make for. Of course, your dog was probably following me. I was in the hut, too.' She did not show it but the thought of a tracker dog following her rather expensive scent amused her.

'Just to set your mind at rest, Madam, there will be a patrol car here tonight and it will stay until we come back in the morning. Be sure to lock up carefully, won't you? And if you should see or hear anything at all suspicious, don't hesitate to call us on this number!' He gave her a slip of paper and bade them goodnight.

'What is going on?' asked Lisa. 'I asked Toby — but he wouldn't tell me anything. Who are they looking for? Is it the man who murdered Mrs Gregory? Is he still hiding in the wood?'

Richard was quite right about his sister. She sounded amazingly cool

— far less upset about the happenings at Greenleafe than Valerie herself. Still — and she thanked heaven for it — the child had not been faced, as she had, with a man she thought she knew who had become a monster before her very eyes.

She was thankful for the children. They seemed to surround her with an atmosphere of sanity — something she needed after a day which had left her feeling drained and sick at heart. More than by the revelation of Simon's true character, she had been driven almost to despair by the look in Toby's eyes. He must really believe that she had been involved in a conspiracy to steal those emeralds — there was no other explanation of the expression on his face or the coldness with which he had spoken to her. She wondered why he had not told the police what he suspected. Perhaps it was out of consideration for the children? In a way, it might have been better if he had told them what he thought. Mr Wagstaff would have been able to confirm that she was Vanessa's twin sister! After all, he had seen them both.

Lisa did not object when, at nine o'clock, Valerie told her to go up to bed. Richard watched television for a little longer but, when the film ended, he said that he too was going to bed, though he intended to read for a while. Valerie was only too glad of the prospect of an early night: she went round the ground floor, making quite certain that all the windows were securely closed and the doors locked and bolted. Now she understood exactly why Mrs Spenser was so security conscious.

When she was satisfied, she went into the kitchen to make a hot drink. There was a slight chill in the air — more than enough, she told herself firmly, to give her that unpleasant shivery feeling. A mug of hot cocoa was just the thing to make her feel better. It was quiet in the kitchen. The only sound was the tick of the old-fashioned clock on the wall.

Disliking the silence and wanting to keep her thoughts from wandering, she switched on the small portable radio on the dresser. It was tuned to Radio 3 and the sudden surge of music comforted her. She turned up the volume: the kitchen walls were so thick that the sound was unlikely to penetrate to the other part of the house and disturb the children.

The milk started hissing in the saucepan before she remembered that she had not fetched either the cocoa or her mug from the pantry. She drew the pan off the hotplate while she went to fetch them. She looked at herself in the mirror which hung beside the pantry door, to see if she looked as washed-out and wan as she was feeling.

'Birthday girl!' she said aloud and put out her tongue at her reflection. In less than five years' time, she told herself, she really would begin to look middle-aged. It would be too late by that time to do anything except struggle on with a career which would never bring her the success she had once hoped for. And now that she had met the one man in the world who made her dreams of stardom seem childish and irrelevant, he had made it perfectly clear that he had no time for her. She had tried to tell herself that Toby was a prig, but it was quite useless. She would have given anything, everything, just for the comfort of being with him. She was in love with him — but, of course, all he felt for her was contempt.

As she looked into the mirror she saw, behind her, the door to the little back staircase. It was starting to open.

'Is that you, Richard?'

'No, my dear. He's fast asleep.' Simon Spenser had swung the door wide open and was standing on the bottom step, smiling at her. Then, before she had a chance to cry out, let alone escape, he bounded across the kitchen and seized her by the shoulders.

'You'd better keep quiet,' he said, 'or I shall kill you.'

'There's no need to be melodramatic,' said Valerie calmly. 'What do you want?'

'I need your help. If you're sensible and do exactly what I ask, I shan't hurt you.'

'How did you get in? All the doors are bolted.'

'Yes, I expect you bolted them all very carefully. I was surprised, this afternoon, when I couldn't get in through the conservatory. I had to wait until you were eating your supper. Then I came in through the back door.'

'But that door was locked!'

'So it was — but you didn't leave the key in the door. I have all my mother's keys. She doesn't need them now . . .'

'Where is she, then?'

Simon giggled; a high-pitched titter which made Valerie shudder. 'Not very far from here!' he said. 'Poor Mama. I thought she'd be pleased to see me, but she wasn't. She's dead.'

'What do you mean?' gasped Valerie. 'That you killed her?'

He smiled impishly. 'She would have sent me back to the clinic,' he said, 'so it's just as well, isn't it? Don't be silly, Valerie — I'm not really sorry. She was an old woman. She'd had her life, so she had no business to rob me of mine . . .'

'But what about the people who saw her leave for the airport?'

He laughed. 'I told you about the other time I played Widow Twankey! So I rang up a car hire firm. Not the one she usually used, the one in her little blue book, but another one altogether. When I took her jewel case to the bank, that was a trial run. It was during the lunch hour so everyone was busy. The girl on the counter hardly spoke to me — just gave me a receipt. Next day, the same driver took me to Kettering railway station. There was no point in going to Heathrow — in any case, there wasn't enough cash in the house. Only just enough to get me to London and back . . .'

'Why come back here?' asked Valerie.

'There were some things I wanted to collect.'

'You took a risk.'

'Oh, yes. But the most awkward part was avoiding the gardener. I was afraid he'd come up to the house the morning Mother was supposed to go away. Luckily he didn't. And it was lucky for me that Mrs Gregory had gone to Lincolnshire for a few days. Not so lucky for her when she came back.'

'But what about your mother?'

'Did you see that great big trunk in the attic? That enormous one . . . my father used it in the tropics. It has a metal lining, to protect the contents from termites. Of course, it's completely air-tight. She's quite safe in there. By the time anybody finds her, I shall be miles away.'

Valerie shuddered. 'Why are you telling me all this?'

'You're not likely to tell anyone else, my dear. Now — what I want you to do is to drive me to the station, first thing tomorrow.'

'Suppose I refuse?'

'You wouldn't do that, Valerie. Because if you did, I should have to kill you. And the children, of course. You wouldn't want that to happen, would you?'

'But everybody would know you'd done it . . .'

'So they would. But I'd be no worse off than I was before. And at least I'd have the pleasure of cutting that little wimp's throat! Being mad — and they all think I'm out of my mind — does give one certain privileges . . .'

'What have you done with the emeralds?'

'They're in a safe place. It's a pity they will have to be left behind, but I wouldn't risk selling them now. Wagglestick will have issued a description of them, now that he knows I'm about. It was a mistake to start looking for that missing drop. Angela's welcome to them, if she can find them. I shall have to make do with the rest of Mother's baubles.

'Make me some black coffee, will you? It won't be getting light for hours and I don't want to risk falling asleep.'

Valerie filled the kettle. Glancing at him, she wondered if she could slip through the kitchen door and get to the telephone in the hall. But he guessed what she was thinking.

'I unplugged the phone and hid it while you were having your supper. And I shouldn't try to wake the children — that would be a fatal mistake.' Again he gave that chilling, high-pitched giggle.

When she turned to face him again, she saw that he had taken a large kitchen knife from the magnetic rack on the wall and was testing the blade with his thumb. Valerie knew how sharp it was; she could hardly ignore such an obvious threat, although she was wondering how much of it was acting, or simply boasting. She did not intend to find out.

'When I get back to London,' he said, 'I shall be able to sell the rest of

Mother's jewellery.'

'How will you get it out of the bank? Surely you can't forge her signature . . .?'

'My dear Valerie, I'm not that stupid! The box in the bank is certainly full of jewellery — there was plenty of theatrical tat in those boxes upstairs. The real stuff I took to London with me.'

'Then why haven't you already sold it?'

'These things take time. You saw that dreadful old anorak I was wearing — it was all I had to put on when I left the clinic. I've had to get some new clothes — I could hardly approach a reputable jeweller looking like a tramp. He'd think I'd stolen the things, wouldn't he? I found enough cash in the house to get me to London and the pittance they gave me in the Portobello Road for the bits and pieces she'd tucked away in her room paid for a few new clothes — but I had to be careful. It's a pity about the emeralds — they're worth more than the rest of the jewellery put together. If I'd kept them in their case, I wouldn't have lost that odd drop. But the case was so big — and it had Mother's monogram on it — and I put the stuff in an old linen shoe bag. It must have had a hole in it . . . '

'How long had you been living in that hut in the wood?'

'Only a few days; it was lucky I knew it was there. It did give me a chance to look for the missing emerald.'

The water was boiling. Luckily there was a jar of instant coffee on the dresser. Valerie took down a decorative mug from one of the hooks: he would hardly allow her out of his sight to let her fetch anything from the pantry.

She was stirring his coffee when the electric bell buzzed loudly. Looking up at the board, she saw the little tell-tale bobbing in the window labelled 'Front Door'.

'You mustn't answer it,' hissed Simon. 'Who do you suppose it is?'

'Probably the police.' Valerie tried to

sound nonchalant. She hoped whoever had rung the bell would go away again. That knife was very sharp — she knew, because she had sharpened it herself — and she was afraid that Simon might be prepared to use it.

Still facing her, the weapon in his hand, he sidled round the room and switched off the radio. The bell buzzed again. Then, in the distance, came a loud hammering on the front door, which went on for some time. Then there was silence.

'I hope whoever it is doesn't come round to the back door,' muttered Simon. 'I think we should go upstairs.'

'What about the light?' asked Valerie, hoping to divert his attention for a moment. 'Shall I switch it off?'

'Stay where you are. I'll do it.' As he went towards the switch, Valerie darted round the table towards the back door.

'Oh, no you don't!' he snarled and was soon close behind her. She picked up the mug of coffee and hurled the scalding liquid into his face. He screamed loudly, dropping the knife, but continued to chase Valerie. Grabbing her by both wrists, he dragged her towards the staircase door, still open as he had left it when he entered the kitchen.

'You little bitch!' he said. 'Now I really am going to kill you!' and he kicked the door open wide and pulled her through it after him. Once more she was amazed by his strength — she had never imagined that he could be as strong as that. It was impossible for her to break free from that grip.

Then she heard voices outside the kitchen door — voices she recognized at once. Toby's deep baritone was unmistakable but so was the other — a woman's voice. The last voice she would have expected to hear at that moment. The kitchen door swung open and she gave a despairing shout as Simon dragged her round the bend in the little staircase, out of sight of the intruders.

Several things happened at once. Simon suddenly let go of her wrists, uttering a peculiar roar as, thrown off balance, she fell down the stairs onto the kitchen floor. A moment later, he fell almost on top of her, landing on his back on the flags, where he lay without moving. He was closely followed by Richard, who was wearing a dressing-gown and brandishing a croquet mallet.

Toby ignored the unconscious Simon and rushed across to Valerie.

'Are you all right? What on earth's going on?' he muttered, putting his arms round her.

Richard, looking very cool, very grown-up in the spotted silk dressing-gown, smiled at the woman who had come into the room with Toby. 'Hello, Mums!' he said. 'Where did you spring from?'

'I think you'd better explain what's happening,' said Vanessa. 'When the plane landed at Heathrow this evening, I thought I'd come straight here and surprise you. But you've managed to surprise me!' She went across to Valerie, who, no longer in Toby's arms, clutched at her sister, hardly able to believe that she was really there.

'Oh, Val!' said Vanessa, 'I've been so worried about you. I've been having the most dreadful nightmares! Of course, when I arrived in Rio, Alex had already gone up country; nobody seemed to know where. There was no chance of finding him, so I decided to stay put and wait for him to come back. But then I changed my mind. I see I was right to be worried — what have you been up to?'

Richard explained. 'I heard voices,' he explained. 'When I went to the bathroom, I saw that someone had left the staircase door open. So I came down to investigate and heard that character threatening Val. He's obviously barmy, but I didn't like the sound of him, so I nipped up to the attic for a weapon. Don't think much of croquet as a game, but this thing turned out to be useful . . . '

'You might have killed him!' said Vanessa.

'It's probably just as well he didn't,' said Toby. 'And it's lucky Mrs Spenser gave me a spare front door key . . . '

'I thought I'd bolted it,' said Valerie.

'Well, if you did, someone must have unbolted it again. Perhaps your friend on the floor?'

'I've told you before — he's not my friend.'

'He seems to be coming round,' said Richard. 'Had I better hit him again?'

'No,' Toby smiled grimly, 'I don't think that's a good idea. Is there any rope? A clothes line, perhaps. Then we'd better tie him up before the police arrive — the patrol car will be round in a few minutes, so we'll stop it and tell them we've got him.'

'I'll fetch the rope!' Richard went towards the utility room, adding gleefully, 'I know some useful knots!'

'Vanessa!' Valerie was puzzled. 'How did you come across Toby?'

'I was watching the house when the car arrived,' Toby explained. 'She drew up and wound down the window

— and then I had a real shock. I thought it was you — I wondered where you'd been and why I hadn't seen you leave the house. And arriving like that in what was obviously a rented car — I thought I was going crazy!'

'And when I asked him exactly where West Lodge was, he looked at me as if I were the crazy one . . .'

'I wonder why I didn't hear the car,' said Valerie.

'You had the radio on very loud!' said Richard, reappearing with the clothes line, eager to demonstrate some of his fancy knots.

When a puzzled and sleepy Lisa wandered into the kitchen, she ignored the man on the floor and stared at Vanessa.

'Oh, my mummy!' she cried, running into her mother's arms.

'My darling,' said Vanessa. 'Everything's all right now. I'm here, and I'm never going away from you again, my darling. I promise — not ever.'

Suddenly Lisa realized that something strange was going on; she saw Toby, with Richard's eager assistance, kneeling on the floor and tying their prisoner's wrists together. Simon was moaning softly but making no attempt to struggle.

'What are you doing to Peter?' Lisa asked angrily. 'Why are you tying him up? He's our friend, isn't he, Valerie?' and she fell on her brother and started to pummel him with her clenched fists.

'Peculiar friends you have, then,' said Vanessa tersely.

11

There was a time when Valerie had loved her little flat. Compact, modern and situated conveniently between the television centre and the West End of London, it had seemed to be the ideal home for an up-and-coming actress. Now it was more like a prison. The rooms were, after all, poky and badly proportioned; the furniture that she had chosen with such care looked shabby and cheap, and the view from the window was of grey buildings, with scarcely a tree in sight. Worst of all, she was oppressed by the constant noise of traffic from the street below. Wistfully, she thought about Greenleafe. In spite of all that had happened there, she longed to be back at West Lodge.

Vanessa had reacted quite differently. When she had heard the whole story, she refused to stay in the house. She swept Valerie and the children off to a hotel in Stirbridge and started to look for somewhere else to live. Being Vanessa, she found another house without much difficulty and moved into it without delay. Valerie helped her to settle in and stayed with the family until Alex returned from Brazil. Then her agent started nagging her about a new television play which, he assured her, was a heaven-sent opportunity. She went back to London, auditioned for the part, was given it and started rehearsals.

She saw nothing of Toby after the night of Vanessa's arrival at Greenleafe. When the police had taken charge of Simon, Toby had slipped away without a word. Later she learned that he had left the district: he had finished his wildlife project and had gone home to Yorkshire to write his report. It was clear to Valerie that he never wanted to see her again.

She tried hard to forget him, but he was never far from her thoughts. When she saw Vanessa and Alex, she realized at last why they were so right together: she must have been blind to think of Alex simply as a dreary, fuddy-duddy cousin, lacking any sort of imagination! Now she could see that, like Toby, Alex was utterly dependable and honest and that he loved Vanessa. Alex's love had enabled him to see through her sister's obvious flightiness to the essential goodness and kindness which were an equally important part of her character.

Lucky Vanessa! If only Toby could have realized that Valerie herself was not the superficial creature he had taken her to be. But he couldn't — and she knew that he never would. To him, she was nothing but a liar and a cheat — and honesty was the quality he admired most. For a moment, when he had rushed across the kitchen and taken her in his arms, she had imagined that he cared for her — until she realized that he would have reacted in the same way to anyone who had just had a bad fright. His abrupt departure from West Lodge that night and the haste with which he had packed up and left Greenleafe proved that he wanted nothing more to do with her.

* * *

Valerie had not been called upon to give evidence at the inquest on Mrs Spenser. She did not attend the court; that was the day when Vanessa had insisted that she should come and look at the new house. It was near Oundle and Vanessa liked it more than she had ever liked West Lodge. It was modern, less isolated and she had been told that the owner might be prepared to sell it to her when the lease expired.

'I didn't know you wanted to buy a house!' said Valerie.

'My wandering days are over,' her sister explained. 'It's time I thought about settling down.' This was so unlike Vanessa that Valerie was more than a little puzzled — until her sister told her that another reason she had decided to return to England, rather than wait for Alex in Rio, was that she had realized she was pregnant — and that, on this occasion, her nesting instinct was stronger than her wanderlust. Of course, Valerie was delighted — and more envious than she would admit, even to herself. Now she knew that she loved a man, it would have been wonderful to have his child. Too bad that he didn't love her.

Of course, Valerie read the report of the inquest. The verdict surprised everybody. When questioned by the police, Simon had soon admitted that the story he told Valerie was a pack of lies. He had not murdered his mother, although he had hidden her body in the trunk. When he arrived at West Lodge after his flight from the clinic, he had found her lying on the sofa in the small sitting-room. Thinking that she was asleep, he had tried to waken her.

He intended to ask her for money; he had the idea that, if he could persuade her that he no longer needed treatment, she would help him to go abroad and start a new life. Then he realized that his mother was dead — she must have died in her sleep.

His first reaction was panic. What was he to do? He had no money: if he ran from the house, it would only be a matter of time before he was picked up and taken back to the clinic. If he stayed where he was and reported her death, he would still have to go back. Then he realized how he might be able to turn what had happened to his own advantage.

His mother had written to tell him about her proposed visit to Angela in Italy. That was partly why he had absconded, for he was worried that she might carry out her threat to give the emeralds to his sister. Naturally, he went through her papers and, finding a letter from Mr Wagstaff about the arrangements for letting West Lodge, he realized that the visit to Italy was to be an extended one.

When the telephone rang, Simon

used his talent for mimicry. A call from the clinic reported his disappearance, so, in his best imitation of his mother's voice, he assured the superintendent that he would let him know at once if the runaway turned up at West Lodge.

His plans became more and more elaborate. He giggled when he recounted how, disguised as his mother, he had deceived the bank cashier and the neighbours who had witnessed 'Mrs Spenser's' departure in the hired car. When he returned secretly to Greenleafe, to find the missing emerald, he decided to live in the hut in the wood until he was ready to dispose of the jewellery.

He did not allow the arrival of Valerie and the children to interfere with his plans. Once or twice, using his mother's keys, he let himself into the house at night, allowing him to search for the emerald in Mrs Spenser's room. On the last of these occasions, he had put the dummy in the bed, guessing that, if she saw it, Lisa would be far too scared to admit that she had been into the locked room. After that, afraid lest his luck should run out and his nocturnal visits be discovered, he had made one or two half-hearted attempts to persuade Valerie to invite him into the house.

He claimed that Mrs Gregory's death had been accidental. It was her own fault, he said, for getting off her bike to talk to him! The money he found in her purse had been a pleasant surprise, helping to keep him going until his plans were ready to put into effect.

Whether he was telling the truth was, in the end, irrelevant. Simon was suffering from a gross mental disorder; he was certified insane and sent to a high security hospital. There was little doubt that he would remain there for the rest of his life.

Mrs Spenser's doctor told the court that she was suffering from a serious heart condition — so serious that he had advised her not to go abroad, as she had planned. Of course, she had refused to take his advice. Her sudden death was not unexpected, so the jury had no difficulty in reaching their verdict — that her death was due to natural causes.

Reading the report in the local paper, Valerie felt almost sorry for Simon. Much sorrier than she felt for his sister, to whom she had taken a violent dislike. The marchesa had gone back to Italy immediately after the funeral, leaving nobody in any doubt that she was far more upset by the loss of the emeralds than by the fate of her mother or her brother.

Valerie had already returned to her flat in London when she realized that she knew where Simon must have hidden the jewels. It was difficult, over the phone, to describe the exact location to Mr Wagstaff, but she told him enough to enable him to find them among the ruins of East Lodge. They were in a hollow, beneath a large stone which had once been a window sill, wrapped, as Simon had told her, in a linen bag. Apart from the missing drop, they were undamaged.

'Won't the marchesa be pleased!' said Valerie, when Mr Wagstaff rang to thank her for her help.

'Perhaps,' said the lawyer drily. He could not have told Valerie more plainly that it was none of her business. Impulsively, she asked him if he had heard from Toby.

'Mr Anderson? Yes, I am expecting to see him in a few days time. Do you want me to give him a message?'

'No, thank you,' said Valerie. 'It really doesn't matter.'

* * *

She was not enjoying the new play. The character she was playing was interesting enough, and it was a larger and more important part than she had ever been given before, but she thought the whole production overloaded and pretentious. After all, she thought, it's really nothing but a cheap little story.

One evening, after a particularly

tiring rehearsal, she came back to her flat feeling thoroughly miserable. Hoping to cheer herself up, she took a hot bath, washed her hair, and put on her favourite housecoat — corded silk in a dull shade of green which showed off the vivid red-gold of her hair. Newly dried, it streamed loose over her shoulders. Wondering whether she had the energy to cook herself a meal or whether it would be less trouble to get dressed again and go out to a restaurant, she was startled by the front doorbell. She picked up the intercom.

'Valerie!' said a deep, unforgettable voice. 'I have to speak to you. May I come up?'

'Toby! What are you doing here?' She did not wait for a reply, but pressed the switch to release the front door and waited to hear his footsteps on the stairs. Then she let him in.

'What are you doing here?' she repeated. 'And why didn't you let me know you were coming?'

'I didn't know myself until this

afternoon. I had to visit a man at the Min of Ag and I wasn't sure how long he'd keep me. Then I tried ringing your number, but a machine answered.'

'You should have left a message. It's infuriating when people just ring off.'

'But I didn't want to talk to a machine, Valerie. I wanted to talk to you. So I decided to come here and surprise you.'

'Supposing I hadn't been here?'

'Then I would have waited outside until you came home.'

'Who gave you my address?'

'Your sister. She wasn't particularly easy to find. I hadn't realized she wasn't going to stay at West Lodge. Luckily Wagstaff knew where she'd gone.'

'Vanessa refused to stay at Greenleafe after what happened.'

'What about you? Do you think the house is haunted?'

'Of course not!' snapped Valerie, 'I think it's a beautiful house. And it's old — it would be very surprising if Mrs Spenser was the first person ever to have died there. In any case, she died peacefully in her sleep. Whatever Simon did afterwards couldn't possibly have hurt her.'

'Very sensible,' said Toby. 'That's exactly how I feel.'

'If I'd been in Vanessa's shoes,' Valerie went on, 'wild horses wouldn't have dragged me away from that gorgeous house! But what do you want to say to me?'

'Just a moment!' Toby looked round the room. 'So this is your home? Not in the least like West Lodge!'

'It's not really my home,' Valerie felt embarrassed. 'It's just somewhere to sleep when I'm working.'

'Rather like my caravan.'

'Yes I suppose it is. Have you still got the caravan? I expect you'll need it when you go on another expedition.'

'Perhaps: it depends. Now I'm no longer working with the Commission, I have moved it. It's in the paddock at West Lodge.'

'And what will happen to West

Lodge? I suppose the marchesa will sell it.'

'No — it's not hers to sell. Mrs Spenser left it to somebody else.' He smiled at her, 'You're looking more beautiful than ever, Valerie. But I'm afraid you've lost weight. I hope you're taking care of yourself.'

'Of course I am. Now, while you're making up your mind what it is you have to say to me, can I get you a cup of tea or coffee? Or a glass of sherry?'

'Not just now,' he said. 'Later!' She raised her eyebrows, wondering how long he intended to stay.

'I've come to apologize,' he said at last.

'What for? For saving my life?'

'It was Richard who did that. No — for being such a clot. I was afraid I'd never see you again.'

'I'm surprised you should want to. You've always made it perfectly clear how much you disapprove of me.'

'Have I? Then I'm even more of an idiot than I thought. The fact is, I've not been completely honest with you.'

'You haven't? Then I'm disappointed. I thought 'honesty' was your middle name.'

'Don't be flippant!' he snapped. 'I've come here to tell you I'm sorry — I don't expect you to poke fun at me.'

'What do you expect me to do? Be as pompous as you are?'

'Valerie. I had almost convinced myself that I disapproved of you.'

'Almost? You completely convinced me.'

'But I had to! You told me you were married. To Alex.'

'No, I didn't. I never actually said I was. But I had to let you believe it, didn't I?'

'I suppose you did. So how could I possibly admit, even to myself, that I'd fallen in love with another man's wife?'

'What did you say? I don't believe that — you're far too level-headed. Even if you did, you soon got over it.'

'That's what I thought,' he sighed.

'So that's that. What was the real

reason you came to see me?'

Toby looked uncomfortable. 'I wanted to ask your advice. Among other things, about West Lodge.'

'What about it?'

'I shall have to make up my mind about it. Whether to live there or somewhere else.'

'Really? Hadn't you better ask the new owner? Who does it belong to, if it isn't the marchesa?'

'It belongs to me. Mrs Spenser left it to me in her will.'

'She couldn't have done! What about her family?'

'They can hardly object. Angela doesn't want it — she received quite a sizeable legacy. And there's a trust to look after Simon's money. Everything else comes to me.'

'I suppose you were much kinder to Mrs Spenser than either of her children . . . '

'Perhaps. Oh, Valerie — I was really fond of that old lady. It's such a pity you never met her . . . '

'You say you're thinking of living in West Lodge? What about your house in Yorkshire?'

'That doesn't belong to me. It's my family home, of course, but eventually it will go to my eldest brother.'

She did not ask him to explain, but waited for him to go on.

'You've already answered one of my questions,' he said. 'So in a moment I'll ask you another. First, I'd better explain. My family isn't particularly rich and, as the youngest son, I've had to choose between doing work I really like — which will never make me a fortune — or doing something more profitable which I wouldn't enjoy. I never thought I should want to marry, so there was no real problem.'

'Wouldn't your wife be prepared to work? Many women do, you know.'

'Yes — I know. But I'm afraid I've always been rather old-fashioned about such things. Particularly if the woman in question earned a great deal more than I did. I don't suppose you understand that point of view. You see, you're the only woman I've met who has had a career that was really important to her. I'd hate to be even partly dependent on my wife . . . but now, with the money I've inherited from Mrs Spenser, and West Lodge, the position's completely changed.'

'I see,' said Valerie, wishing he would get to the point.

'Of course,' he said suddenly, 'you are wrong about one thing. West Lodge *is* haunted!'

'What do you mean?'

'It's haunted by a girl with red hair. When Wagstaff gave me the keys and I went to look round by myself, I saw her everywhere. She was in the kitchen, with icing sugar all over her hands — and her nose. It made her nose look sweeter than ever — I remember how much I wanted to kiss it! In the garden, I saw her playing croquet with the children. I'd come to have a word with Bagster and I caught a glimpse of her. She didn't even know I was there. And in the little sitting-room, sizzling with anger, looking ten times more aristocratic than that ridiculous Angela. You were everywhere, Valerie. I couldn't move a step without seeing you.'

'You're making all this up!' she protested. He only laughed.

'Perhaps I am. But it was you who told me that there is more than one kind of truth. And you've taught me to see things differently, too. I understand, now, that your career is just as important to you as mine is to me. If I'm prepared to wait patiently at home while you weave your enchantment over your audience, and try not to feel jealous or hard done by — will you marry me, Valerie?'

For the last few minutes, Valerie had been almost certain that that was what he had been leading up to — but, now she had heard him say the actual words, the idea came as a shock.

'Marry you?' she said. 'Are you sure? You hardly know me.'

'I know you well enough to realize

that I want to spend the rest of my life getting to know you better! You — and all the other characters you will be playing. Wondering how much of each of them is you and how much is simply . . . '

'Lies?' She finished the sentence for him.

'I was going to say imagination.'

She sighed. 'I have a confession to make. I used to enjoy acting, but it's no longer the most important thing in my life. The magic has worn off. I've been reasonably lucky and I've enjoyed myself a lot. But the time has come to give it up.'

'Just as I've got used to the idea?' asked Toby.

'Why? Are you disappointed?'

He did not reply and she wondered what he was thinking. Her mind raced; he had asked her to marry him, implied that he wanted her to live with him at Greenleafe — the two things she wanted most in the world. So what was wrong?

'Those emeralds,' he said gloomily.

'What about them? Don't they belong to the marchesa now?'

'No. Mrs Spenser left them to me. She mentioned them specifically in her will. The obvious thing to do would be to sell them — there's an animal protection society I'm interested in who would make very good use of the money I'd get for them. But now I'm not sure . . . '

'What's the problem?'

'I should like to see you wearing them!' he said, almost angrily. 'The tiara, glowing against the flame of your hair. That necklace, setting off your white neck and your beautiful shoulders — the emeralds would make your eyes look greener than ever . . . You'd look so incredibly beautiful, Valerie!'

She shuddered. She had never seen Mrs Spenser's emeralds, apart from the photograph and the pendant Lisa had mistakenly given to her. She had often imagined wearing jewels like that. She knew, without vanity but with the unself-conscious objectivity of an actress that she would look every bit as beautiful as Toby imagined. Yet now, the idea filled her with horror. When she thought of the emeralds, she could see only the mad gleam in Simon's eyes and the avaricious glint in Angela's.

'Why couldn't she have left them to her daughter?' she blurted out angrily.

'Because, when it came to the point, she didn't want to. She realized that Angela only wanted them for the money they'd make. I want to see you wearing them, my darling.'

'When?' Valerie looked into his eyes. Then she laughed, 'When I'm bathing our children? Honestly, Toby, the animal trust would make far better use of them.'

It only took a moment for him to realize what she had said. Then she was in his arms and they were both laughing and kissing each other, looking ahead to the happy years they would spend together. Emeralds didn't matter, thought Valerie. Nor money, nor even West Lodge itself. All they needed, they would find in each other — and that was the real truth.

THE END

Other titles in the
Linford Romance Library:

CONVALESCENT HEART

Lynne Collins

They called Romily the Snow Queen, but once she had been all fire and passion, kindled into loving by a man's kiss and sure it would last a lifetime. She still believed it would, for her. It had lasted only a few months for the man who had stormed into her heart. After Greg, how could she trust any man again? So was it likely that surgeon Jake Conway could pierce the icy armour that the lovely ward sister had wrapped about her emotions?

TOO MANY LOVES

Juliet Gray

Justin Caldwell, a famous personality of stage and screen, was blessed with good looks and charm that few women could resist. Stacy was a newcomer to England and she was not impressed by the handsome stranger; she thought him arrogant, ill-mannered and detestable. By the time that Justin desired to begin again on a new footing it was much too late to redeem himself in her eyes, for there had been too many loves in his life.

MYSTERY AT MELBECK

Gillian Kaye

Meg Bowering goes to Melbeck House in the Yorkshire Dales to nurse the rich, elderly Mrs Peacock. She likes her patient and is immediately attracted to Mrs Peacock's nephew and heir, Geoffrey, who farms nearby. But Geoffrey is a gambling man and Meg could never have foreseen the dreadful chain of events which follow. Throughout her ordeal, she is helped by the local vicar, Andrew Sheratt, and she soon discovers where her heart really lies.

HEART UNDER SIEGE

Joy St Clair

Gemma had no interest in men — which was how she had acquired the job of companion/secretary to Mrs Prescott in Kentucky. The old lady had stipulated that she wanted someone who would not want to rush off and get married. But why was the infuriating Shade Lambert so sceptical about it? Gemma was determined to prove to him that she meant what she said about remaining single — but all she proved was that she was far from immune to his devastating attraction!

HOME IS WHERE THE HEART IS

Mavis Thomas

Venetia had loved her husband dearly. Now she and their small daughter were living alone in a beautiful, empty home. Seeking fresh horizons in a Northern seaside town, Venetia finds deep interest in work with a Day Centre for the Elderly — and two very different men. If ever she could rediscover love, would Terry bring it with his caring, healing laughter? Or would it be Jay, the once well-known singer now at the final crossroads of his troubled career?

O.K.Z.

THE ELUSIVE DOCTOR

Claire Vernon

Wearing spectacles to make herself appear more dignified, twenty-year-old Candy gained the longed-for post as secretary to the two principals of a school in the African mountains. She was often overworked, sometimes shocked, occasionally unhappy. But all through her days at the school there ran a single thread, which bound her to the one person with whom she felt most at ease, the man who finally said unforgivable, hurtful things — the man she could not forget.